ABDUCTED!

A SHERIFF REYNOLDS MYSTERY

DEBBIE MUMFORD

WDM
Publishing

COPYRIGHT

PRAISE FOR DEBBIE MUMFORD

Praise for *Delectable Mountain Quilting*:

LW from Amazon: Five stars: *"Will read more of the series. Love quilting and related stuff. Story was gripping and well constructed."*

———

Jean from Amazon: Five stars: *"I enjoyed the easy read. A nice story with likable people. I used to quilt, so I understand the value of the antique quilt."*

———

Praise for *In a Pickle*:

Quilter from Amazon: Five stars: *"I'm a quilter and throughly enjoyed this story. I like a good series like this second book."*

———

Norrine B from Amazon: Five stars: *"Kept you on the edge of your seat. Good book for a snowy day in front of a fireplace with a warm beverage."*

———

Praise for *Second Sight*:

Bookgirl from Amazon: Five stars: "A lost love, a new love, psychic magic, a murder and a tiger! Wow. I loved this book. It was fast paced and easy to read. I got caught up in the "I'll just read one more chapter" syndrome and lost a bit of sleep but it was worth it. I hope Ms. Mumford writes more in this world. I love these characters."

———

Dragon Slayer from Amazon: Five stars: "I liked the characters and the story line. For those that love a mystery and a good romance along with the paranormal, this book is for you."

———

Praise for *Sorcha's Heart*
Katie from Goodreads: Five stars: 'This story was fantastic...I strongly recommend anyone who likes paranormal dragon stories read this. Best prequel ever. Off to look for more by this author."

———

Old Ozark Gal from Amazon: Five stars: "...for those who enjoy a sizzling relationship without the graphic descriptions of what body part goes where, this is an excellent book. So what are you waiting for? Go read it!"

———

Karyn-Anne from Amazon: Five stars: "The romantic scenes were full of passion and heat, but not graphic or explicit. I really, really enjoyed this novella ... Very highly recommended!"

———

Ahmari from Amazon: Five stars: "This book is very well written ... I liked it so much I purchased the sequel! ... a unique idea for a fantasy and told in a delightful manner. I look forward to reading more from this author."

———

Praise for _Her Highland Laird:_

Katharina from Amazon: Five stars: "I'm normally not someone who reads romance novels, but ... I stumbled over Debbie Mumford's Romance stories. This one was an absolute treat. Not only did it depict the life in 15th century correctly (well researched for such a short story), it evokes emotion very well ... I'll definitely read more by this author."

———

Tony from Amazon: Five stars: "Very interesting story. With some suspense and an interesting thread of love."

LORI RICHARDSON

Lorelei Richardson breathed a contented sigh as she stared eastward toward the foothills of her beloved Absaroka Mountains. She'd missed the 'Sorkees terribly and had ridden out from her father's ranch, the Circle R, before breakfast that morning to convince herself that she was truly home, that her freshman year of college was actually over. Lori knew Billings, Montana wasn't a huge city—not compared to New York or Chicago or even Denver—but for a girl raised on a ranch in the Montana's Paradise Valley, life in any city was a major adjustment.

Now she sat astride Beauty, the buckskin mare she'd raised from a foal, with the morning breeze sifting through her shoulder-length chestnut hair and the sun warm on her freckled face.

God, it was good to be home!

She was just about to turn Beauty toward the ranch house and breakfast when she noticed two men following Garnet Creek out of the canyon its waters had carved. Puzzled, she reined Beauty in and watched the men approach. Tall, husky men in their forties, both wore flannel shirts, jeans, and hiking boots. Faded ball caps covered their close-shorn heads. She didn't recognize either and she should have; she knew everyone in this valley.

The fact that both men carried rifles worried her as well. It wasn't hunting season, especially not in the 'Sorkees, which were under Federal protection. And why were they on foot? Sure, lots of people hiked in the 'Sorkees, but they did so from designated trails, not by traipsing across private ranch lands.

Best not take chances.

She'd set her heels to Beauty's flanks and reined her toward the house when a rifle report sounded and a clod of dirt exploded in Beauty's path. The mare shied and pranced back several feet, but though her skin quivered, she didn't rear. Lori had trained her well.

"Hold up there, little lady," the man who hadn't yet raised his rifle called. "That's a fine looking animal. I'd hate for Bart here to have to shoot it."

"Who are you and what right do you have to threaten me or my mare?" Lori's anger burned right through her fear. How dare they threaten Beauty! And on Lori's family's land. "You're on private lands and you need to leave. Now."

Bart kept his rifle aimed at Beauty's chest while the other man strode forward and grabbed her bridle.

"Climb down," the man holding the bridle said. "If Bart shoots your horse and you're still in the saddle, you might break a leg in the fall." He grinned, but it wasn't a pleasant expression. "We'd be hard pressed to get you back to camp on a busted pin."

Lori scowled. "Camp? What camp?"

"Enough talk," Bart called, his rifle still cocked and aimed. "You'll find out everything you need to know when we're back at camp. Now do as Darrin says and get off that damn horse."

Darrin shrugged. "We can do this the easy way or the hard way, but whichever you're coming with us."

Lori bit her lip. She'd let them get too close. She was sure Beauty could wrench her head away from Darrin if Lori asked it, but the mare would probably be shot. And Lori had no way of knowing if the horse would survive. But if Bart missed or only winged Beauty, they could outrun the men and make it back to the ranch house. She'd call the sheriff. She and her father and brothers could hold off two men while Sheriff Reynolds and his deputies sped to the ranch.

But if Beauty went down, which seemed entirely too likely, Lori would be taken, possibly injured. And if Beauty died… well, it might be a while before anyone found her carcass. The Circle R was a big spread and Lori hadn't told anyone where she intended to ride.

No, if Lori was going to be taken, her best chance at rescue was for Beauty to return riderless. That would raise the alarm and folk would come looking for Lori. She just had to make sure she left a clear trail for them to follow.

"Fine," she said, shifting her weight to her left leg and swinging her right over Beauty's back. "No need to shoot my horse. What do you want anyway?"

She stepped out of the stirrup, found her balance on the stiff pasture grass, and patted Beauty's shoulder.

Darrin released Beauty's bridle and grabbed Lori's arm. "You." He jerked his head toward Bart, who lowered his rifle. "Lookie here, Bart. We've got ourselves a pretty woman. She's going to make our camp a hell of a lot more comfortable."

Bart grinned. "That's the God's honest truth. Can you cook, girl?"

She scowled at them. "What do you think? I'm ranch raised."

Bart nodded. "Let's move out."

Before Darrin could drag her toward the canyon, Lori managed to swat Beauty on the rump and yell, "Go home, girl!"

Bart swung his rifle up. The horse had bolted, but was still in range. He fired once. Beauty stumbled and nearly went down. Another shot cracked the morning stillness, and Beauty fell.

Lori wrenched away from Darrin and ran to her horse.

"Beauty!" she cried as she knelt beside the dying animal. "I'm so sorry," she whispered as she stroked her faithful mare's nose. Beauty's flanks quivered, and on a final exhale, the mare died.

Lori jumped to her feet and screamed, "You killed my horse!"

Darrin grabbed her again, slapped her, and dragged her toward the canyon. "Let's move, Bart. We don't know there wasn't someone close enough to hear those shots."

Tears filled Lori's eyes as she glanced at Beauty. Her face stung from the slap, but she'd suffered worse pains working on the ranch. Gamely she gritted her teeth and yanked her arm out of Darrin's hold. Turning, she ran, managing only a few steps before the butt of Bart's rifle hit the back of her head and her world went black.

SHERIFF REYNOLDS

Sheriff Jason Reynolds strode into the single story white stucco building that housed the Garnet County Sheriff's Department. A tall, well-muscled man with a high forehead, strong jaw and steely gray eyes, he nodded to the deputy on duty. The younger man sat at the high wooden counter that separated the public portion of the room from the area where Jason's staff worked. Jason headed straight to his office.

Closing his office door behind himself, he glanced around the small room. It wasn't much to look at— a little on the dingy side, with pale green walls, an old-fashioned wooden teacher's desk, a pair of gray metal filing cabinets, and an overflowing bookshelf— but it was his and he was proud to occupy it. Proud to be trusted enough by the citizens of Garnet County, Montana to hold this elected office.

Taking off his official Stetson cowboy hat, he hung it on the coat rack beside the window. Moving to his desk he settled into the ancient rolling desk chair and pulled over a stack of paper-work. Sometimes he thought the forms and reports bred in his inbox overnight, like oversexed rabbits. Sighing, he got to work. He loved his job, but he preferred solving crimes to writing reports about them or balancing the department's too often tight budget. Still, he had a good staff and a team of fine deputies. When they put reports on his desk, it was his duty— and his privilege— to read them.

He'd just signed off of Eric Lawson's report of a bungled robbery when a knock sounded on his door.

"Come," he called as he shifted Deputy Lawson's report to the to-be-filed pile. The door opened and his second in command, Chief Deputy Janet Millson, stepped inside. An attractive woman, Deputy Millson was nearing thirty with a rich coppery complexion and dark eyes that gleamed with intelligence... and occasionally mischief. She wore her dark hair pulled into a no-nonsense knot at the back of her neck and her uniform was always crisp and spotless.

"Sorry to bother you, Jason, but I wanted to let you know that I'm hosting a barbecue at my place this Saturday. I'm hoping you and Kristi will come."

Jason leaned back in his chair and ran his fingers through his wavy chestnut hair. "I'll check with Kristi, but I don't think we have anything going on this weekend. We'd love to come. Can we bring anything?"

Janet grinned. "Just yourselves."

Nodding, Jason said, "Great. I'll let you know for sure once I've cleared it with Kristi."

Giving him a thumbs-up, Janet left the office, closing the door behind herself.

Jason glanced at his in-box. He'd made good progress on the paperwork. All but two of the reports had been transferred to the to-be-filed stack. Deciding he'd earned a break, he stood, stretched, and stared out of his window. It was a gorgeous day with brilliant sunshine, blue sky, and only a few puffy white clouds. He felt like he could see forever. Montana was Big Sky Country indeed!

Turning away from the window, he reached for his cell

phone. Might as well call his wife right now and get Janet's barbecue on their calendar. He smiled. His wife. Six months into their renewed marriage and he still felt almost giddy every time he thought about Kristi as his wife.

They'd been married before, but Jason had lost her when he'd had a fling with a stranger at an out-of-state conference. Kristi wasn't a woman to put up with infidelity; she'd divorced him immediately. He'd lost the love of his life over a bit of sex that he hadn't even enjoyed. It had taken nearly losing her to a felon's bullet to wake him up and make him realize that whether she forgave him or not, Kristi was the only woman for him.

Fortunately, that bullet had also reminded Kristi that Jason was the man she would always love. It had taken him a year and half after that fateful event, but he'd won her trust again and they'd remarried last Thanksgiving.

He grinned as he held the cell phone to his ear and waited for her to answer. Calling his wife for something as mundane as checking their calendar. He was a lucky man!

"Hi, handsome," she said when she answered. "What's up?"

"Hey, love. Janet just invited us to a barbecue Saturday night. Does that work for you?"

"Just a sec. I don't think of anything else we have going on, but let me check the calendar."

He waited patiently. Kristi was nearly as busy as he was, being the owner of a successful quilt shop. Plus, she often taught classes for her customers, but those were usually held on week nights. They both tried to keep their weekends free.

A moment later she said, "All clear. I've put it on our schedule. What should we take?"

He laughed. "You'll be proud. I actually remembered to ask her that."

"And…" Kristi prompted.

"She said just to bring ourselves."

"Perfect," Kristi said with a giggle. "I can manage that."

"My thought exactly."

"Anything else?"

"Just a reminder that I love you," Jason said, his voice going low and husky.

"And I love you."

Jason had barely returned his cell phone to his pocket, when his intercom beeped. Flipping it on, he said, "What is it, Clara?"

"Sheriff, I have Ethan Richardson on the line," Clara replied. His dispatcher and occasional secretary, Clara kept the whole department running smoothly. "Do you have a moment to speak with him?"

Jason sat back down and reached for his desk phone. "Of course. Put him through, Clara."

"He's on line one, Sheriff."

Jason punched the blinking light and said, "This is Sheriff Reynolds. How can I help you, Ethan?"

3

ETHAN RICHARDSON

E than Richardson wasn't a man who flustered easily. He was ranch born and bred. He and his younger brother had grown to manhood on the Circle R, but their paths had separated when they went to college. Ethan had gone to Bozeman to attend Montana State University, earning a degree in Agricultural Business with a concentration in ranch management. Teddy had chosen the University of Montana in Missoula where he'd excelled in their Family Medicine program.

Ethan had also found the love of his life in Bozeman. Amanda Collins had been an art student, and, luckily for Ethan, she'd fallen in love with him as well. They'd married during their junior year and had begun their life together.

After college, Ethan and Amanda had returned to the Circle R to work with his father until his parents had retired to Florida, leaving the ranch in Ethan's more than capable hands. Now his sons, Luke and Charlie, carried on the family tradition.

No, Ethan wasn't a worrier. He was a worker. But this morning his gut told him something was wrong. Just as it had before his beloved Amanda had died in a rafting accident on the Yellowstone River. He might not borrow trouble by worrying, but he paid attention to his instincts, and this morning they were buzzing with warning.

His youngest, Lorelei—who was the spitting image of her dead mother—had just returned to the ranch after completing her freshman year of college in Billings, but she hadn't turned up for breakfast. When they were home, their family always started the day together before heading off to their individual tasks. Lori wouldn't shirk the family tradition.

Ethan had searched the ranch house while Luke and Charlie had checked the outbuildings. No sign of her, though Luke had reported that Lori's mare was also missing. Fine. She'd gone for an early ride. Nothing unusual about that... Ethan knew she'd missed both the ranch and her mare.

But she wouldn't have missed breakfast.

Luke and Charlie had ridden out as soon as the meal was done. They'd planned to ride fence today anyway, now they would keep an eye out for their younger sister as well.

Ethan had learned to trust his gut long ago, so even though he knew the sheriff wouldn't be able to do anything yet he settled at his desk, picked up the receiver on the landline, and dialed the Garnet County Sheriff's Department.

The dispatcher answered after only one ring. "Sheriff's office, Clara speaking." Ethan smiled. He'd known Clara Dahl since childhood and she had always been an on-the-ball kind of gal.

"Morning, Clara. This is Ethan Richardson. Is the sheriff there? I need to speak to him."

"Just a moment, Ethan. I'll check to see if he's free."

Elevator music drifted across the phone line as Ethan waited. He hated that sound; he'd prefer silence. Hopefully it wouldn't last long. He drummed his fingers on his desk and worked to avoid gritting his teeth. His daughter was missing, and he was listening to elevator music!

"This is Sheriff Reynolds. How can I help you, Ethan?"

Ethan blew out the breath he hadn't realized he'd been

holding and said, "Thanks for taking my call, Sheriff. I think my daughter, Lorelei, is missing."

"You think?"

"It looks like she went for a ride before breakfast, but she hasn't come back yet."

"What's it been, Ethan? An hour or two?"

Ethan sighed. "Something like that." He could almost see the sheriff shaking his head.

"I'm sorry, Ethan, but there's nothing we can do until she's been gone for twenty-four hours. Give me a call tomorrow if she doesn't show up."

Just as the sheriff was about to end the call, Ethan's cell phone rang. He'd purposely used the landline to keep his cell available in case one of Lori's brothers found anything.

"Hold on a second, Sheriff," he said quickly. "One of my boys is calling." Grabbing his cell, he accepted the call.

"Dad. This is Luke. I found Beauty. She's been shot. The mare is dead."

Fear turned Ethan's gut to ice. If Beauty had been killed, what happened to Lori?

"Hold on, son. I have the sheriff on the other line." Picking up the receiver, he told Sheriff Reynolds about Luke's discovery.

After a moment's pause, the sheriff said, "That changes things, Ethan." Reynolds voice was brisk. He was all business now. "One of my deputies and I will be right there. Tell your son not to trample the area; there may be evidence we can gather."

Ethan nodded. "I'll do that, and... thank you, Sheriff."

"We'll be there as soon as we can, Ethan. Sit tight. Don't do anything until we get there."

4

SHERIFF REYNOLDS

After ending the call with Ethan Richardson, Sheriff Jason Reynolds strode out of his office, his expression serious. He stood with fists on hips as he surveyed his team.

"Listen up, everyone," he called. "We have a developing situation out at the Circle R— the Richardson ranch."

"What's up, Jason?" Janet Millson asked.

"A possible abduction of Richardson's college-age daughter."

A sharp intake of breath circled the room and attention sharpened.

"What's your plan?" Janet asked. As his second-in-command, she often spoke for the whole team.

"I'm not sure yet. I need to get out there and examine the scene." He paused, then nodded as if to himself. "Janet, I'll need you here to keep the department running and to coordinate whatever I determine needs to happen next."

She nodded. "You got it."

"Eric, I'll want you with me." He paused for a moment, considering. "You too, Adam."

Deputy Adam Brooks was new to Jason's team. He'd come highly recommended from the Missoula office. At thirty-five, he was older than most new hires, but his resume and recommendations were stellar. This would be Jason's first opportunity to work with him in the field. Plus, his tracking skills were reputed to be outstanding. If this really was an abduction, Adam might be exactly the man they needed to find the Richardson girl quickly.

"Everyone else," Jason continued, "business as usual unless Janet says differently." He stepped back to his office to grab his Stetson, but turned to add, "Eric, grab a sat phone in case we move out of cell phone range." A satellite phone could be invaluable if the search took them into the 'Sorkees. Better to have it and not need it than to wish he did.

Settling his Stetson on his head, he called, "Eric, Adam, let's roll."

Twenty minutes later, the three law men joined the Richardson men on horseback. Luke led the group to the remains of Lori's horse. Ethan filled Jason in as they rode.

"Luke rode back to the house," Ethan explained. "He didn't like it, he wanted to rush off looking for Lori, but I insisted he come back. Leave the site as untrampled as possible for you and your men."

Jason nodded. "Appreciate that. I know it was hard, but it was the right call."

As the mare's corpse came into view, Jason called out. "Hold up, everyone. Let's keep these horses at a distance. Don't want to destroy evidence under their hooves."

Jason swung out of his saddle and handed his reins to Ethan. Eric and Adam followed suit.

"Adam, take the lead," Jason said.

Adam nodded and studying the land before him walked slowly and carefully toward the dead animal. Jason and Eric followed. Once beside the carcass, Adam circled the animal then spiraled outward, looking for tracks, while Jason and Eric knelt to examine the mare.

"Looks like she was taken out with two thirty-aught-six rounds," Jason called to the Richardson men.

"Sheriff," Adam said, examining the ground near the mare's head, "there's sign of a scuffle here," he pointed to the ground "and tracks leading off in that direction," he gestured toward the stream and a narrow canyon.

Jason stood. "Right. Let's see where they lead." Turning to the Richardsons, he said, "Ethan, you can have your men remove the carcass. If possible, see that the bullets are dug out and sent to my people. We'll have the crime lab run some tests and see what they can tell us."

"I'll do that, Sheriff," Ethan said, pulling out his cell phone, "but if you're tracking these bastards, my boys and I want to come along."

"Someone needs to deal with the horses," Jason began, hoping to discourage Lori's family's participation.

"Charlie and Luke can picket them near the creek. The ranch hands who come out to deal with the mare can take them back to the stable. I'll ask them to leave us a couple of four-wheelers for when we're ready to head back."

Jason pulled off his Stetson and wiped his forehead on the sleeve of his khaki uniform shirt. He didn't want the Richardson men along, but he could see by their grim expressions that they would follow whether he wanted them or not. Best to keep them where he could see them and knew what they were doing. Angry men didn't make the best choices.

"Fine," he said. "Make your arrangements while Deputy Brooks and I get the lay of the land. Deputy Lawson, call in to the station and let Chief Deputy Millson know what's going on."

5

LORI RICHARDSON

L ori stumbled but managed to catch her balance before the man behind her could touch her. She was hot and sweaty from tramping along what was undoubtedly a game trail leading her deeper into the wilderness of the Absaroka Mountains. With her hands tied in front of her, keeping her balance was becoming more challenging as the trail steepened.

"You're going to wish you hadn't done this," she said, anger coloring her voice. "My father and brothers will come for me, and when they find you…"

The man behind her shoved her—Bart. That was his name. The beast who had killed Beauty—causing her to stumble and almost fall. Catching herself on a sagebrush, she managed to break a twig without tearing it off. When Bart didn't notice what she'd done, Lori determined to leave as many trail markers as she could manage. Dad and Luke and Charlie would find her… and she intended to help them do it.

"*If* they show up, they'll die," he growled. "Just like that buckskin of yours."

Darrin, the man leading the way, turned and walked backwards a few paces. "Leave her be, Bart. She'll lose hope soon enough." He let his gaze travel over Lori's body with leering appreciation. "In the meantime, a little defiance will spice things up."

Bart chuckled and shoved her again. "Yeah, we'll have fun breaking her. Women are just like horses and dogs. They need to learn to obey."

Lori seethed at their innuendos, but kept her mouth shut. Beneath her veneer of anger, she was terrified. But she held on to the rage as a shield. She had to, because if her anger slipped, she might dissolve into a puddle of gibbering fear.

Her father and brothers would come. These horrible men who had killed her horse and dragged her through the canyon into the 'Sorkees would pay. She just had to hold on long enough for her family to find her.

After slogging through the creek and then along the game trail for what felt like hours, she finally broke the silence.

"Where are you taking me?"

"We've got a nice little camp," Darrin said over his shoulder. "You're going to make it right homey."

She sniffed. "As if!"

Bart snickered. "You will, once we've taught you some manners." He closed the gap between them and ran a finger down the back of her neck. "I'm going to enjoy breaking you. Just wait until I get you naked. You'll be begging me…"

"That's enough, Bart," Darrin said. "No need to get her all hot and bothered before it's time to bed her down."

Lori shivered, hoping Bart wouldn't notice. But he'd moved back to his previous position, a few strides behind her. Her heart raced, thumping so hard she was sure it would break a rib.

They intended to rape her.

Of course they did.

She'd known that the moment they'd taken her, but having the intention spoken aloud gave it a reality that increased her terror. She wrung her hands, working at the ropes binding her wrists and rubbing her skin raw. If she could just free herself...

What?

Sure, she likely knew the terrain better than these horrible men, but could she outrun a bullet? She was fast— she'd been on the track team in high school, but she wasn't as fast as Beauty. And speed hadn't saved her mare.

But she had to escape. She just had to! No way would she allow these perverts to rape her. She hadn't slept with Billy Walters, and she really liked him. No. Her first sexual experience couldn't be rape! It just couldn't.

Her dad and Luke and Charlie were coming. They'd notice the broken twigs she was leaving. They'd find her.

She held on to that thought, chanting it like a mantra in her mind. *They're coming. They'll find me.*

Nothing else was an acceptable outcome.

At long last Darrin stopped. Bart stepped up beside her and pushed her to sit on a fallen log beside the trail. Darrin hunkered down in front of her, pulled his backpack off his shoulders and reached inside. He handed her a canteen. "Drink."

Unscrewing the lid, Lori sniffed the contents before taking a mouthful of tepid water. Darrin grabbed the canteen away before she could drink more and gulped some for himself.

Bart settled beside her on the log, too close for her comfort, and drank from his own canteen.

"Not far now," Darrin said, glancing at the sky. "We'll be in camp in time for lunch."

Bart bumped his shoulder against Lori's. "You can rustle up something for us to eat," he said. "Unless you'd rather strip down and show us what we got?"

Lori's cheeks flamed and she stared at the ropes binding her wrists. If only she could ignite them with a thought. Better yet, if only she could geld Bart with her mind!

"Patience, Bart," Darrin said. "We've got all the time in the world to hump our little prize. First we need to get our camp in order."

They're coming. They'll find me. They're coming. They'll find me. Lori filled her mind with her mantra.

And when they do, I'll make these two sorry they ever saw me!

6

SHERIFF REYNOLDS

By the time the Richardsons and Deputy Lawson had completed their tasks, Jason and Adam Brooks had tracked the kidnappers to the entrance to the narrow canyon Garnet Creek had carved from the native bedrock. Jason had been sure the men had retreated through that canyon—it was the only reasonable path they could take dragging an unwilling girl with them—but it was good to have his notion confirmed by Adam's tracking skills.

When the other men joined them, Jason weighed his options. He could hold here, contact Janet and have her assemble a search party of his other deputies and National Park Service law enforcement rangers, or he could lead the men he had through that canyon and into the 'Sorkees on his own.

Assembling the larger manhunt was smarter, but it would take time, and he knew Lori's father and brothers would want her back as soon as possible. Truth be told, so did Jason. He didn't like to think what those men might do to the young woman given time and opportunity. He wanted her safely back to her family with as little trauma as possible.

So, he didn't dither. He made what he hoped was the best decision.

"All right. Adam here has determined that they went through this canyon." He glanced at Ethan Richardson and nodded. "We're going to follow. Eric, give Janet another call. Ask her to assemble a search party. Make sure law enforcement rangers are included. We'll let her know where to deploy once everyone is assembled and ready." He paused, staring into the creek's rushing waters before adding, "And ask her to have Clara contact Kristi and let her know what's going on."

"You got it, Sheriff." Eric pulled out the sat phone and got busy relaying the boss's orders.

"Ethan, Luke, Charlie, here's what we're going to do. Adam and I will take the lead. You three will stay behind us. Eric will bring up the rear. If we lose the trail, we'll split into three groups. No one wanders off alone. I'll assign partners if and when it becomes necessary." Jason nodded to Adam. "Let's move out."

The walls of the canyon were steep and the creek's bank disappeared quickly. Soon the men had to remove their footwear and slog through the water. Despite being June, the water was icy cold, runoff from last winter's snow. Before long Jason's feet ached from the cold, but they kept moving. At last, the canyon ended and they stepped gratefully into a little glade surrounded by aspen, chokecherry, and juniper trees. Beyond those, Jason could see the towering Ponderosa pines.

The men settled to the ground, dried their feet, and replaced their socks and boots.

Adam, the first on his feet again, was busily scouring the ground for signs of their quarry.

"Anything?" Jason asked, getting to his own feet again.

Adam didn't bother looking up. "Not yet, but I doubt they'd have wanted to stay in the stream any longer than we did."

Jason nodded. "Agreed." He turned to the others. This wasn't a group of hikers out for a day's trek. None of them had proper supplies, but he'd noticed that each of the Richardsons had a canteen. Undoubtedly pulled from their saddlebags when they'd tethered their horses. "If you have iodine tablets in your pocket, you might want to refill those canteens before we move out."

Ethan nodded and pulled a small vial from his pocket. "We'll do that."

Just then, Adam let out a whoop. "Got 'em!" He stood with a grin on his face. "They went this way."

Jason nodded, noted that everyone was on their feet, and said, "Let's move."

Adam took the lead again, moving toward a stand of chokecherry trees. Once under the cover of the trees' canopy, he pointed ahead. "They seem to be following a game trail, but watch your feet, the undergrowth can still trip you up."

Though it wasn't yet noon, by the time they reached the pine forest the light was dim and their progress slowed. Sunlight filtered through the branches of the tall trees, but the shrubbery around them cut out even more light before it had the chance to reach the ground. Adam was diligent in his tracking, ensuring that the men they followed hadn't moved off the narrow game trail, and Jason was also studying the sign of their passage. But with their attention focused on the ground, they might have missed a few clues if it weren't for Luke.

"Sheriff," Luke called. "I think Lori is leaving us breadcrumbs."

Jason stopped, frowning. "What? I haven't noticed any bread or crusts."

Luke gave a wry laugh. "Not literal breadcrumbs. See here?" He pointed to a broken twig on a sagebrush bush. "I noticed another a few yards back on a rabbitbrush bush."

"Good girl," Jason whispered. He looked up and met Ethan's gaze. "She's smart, your daughter. And this is good news. She's alive and alert enough to think about leaving us a trail."

Ethan nodded. "She's not hurt... at least she's not hurt bad." His gaze turned hard. "If they hurt her..."

Jason interrupted Ethan's words. "Leave that thought alone, Ethan. We're going to get Lori back and we're going to send her kidnappers to prison. For now, let's keep following the trail she's left us."

7

CHIEF DEPUTY JANET MILLSON

C hief Deputy Sheriff Janet Millson stared at the topographical map she'd pinned to the whiteboard they typically used as a murder board. She fervently hoped this case wouldn't turn into a murder. Tracing the line through the canyon at the edge of the Richardson ranch, she noted the elevations Jason, Eric, and the new deputy, Adam, were dealing with. Not too bad. At least, not yet. Depending on where the hunt took them, they could be heading into some pretty wild territory.

Of course, that was the beauty of the Absaroka Mountains. Untamed and potentially dangerous if you didn't know what you were doing or were unprepared.

The Sheriff and his deputies knew what they were doing, but they hadn't gone out to the Circle R prepared for a trek into the wilderness. It was her job to make sure those who joined them were prepared.

"Okay everyone, listen up," she said turning to the remaining deputies as well as both their dispatcher, Clara Dahl, and her back-up, Anita Spencer. "This is an *all hands on deck* situation. We have a young woman who has been kidnapped and taken into the 'Sorkees. Jason and Eric and Adam are on the trail along with the victim's father and two brothers. If all goes well, no one else will be joining the manhunt."

Deputy Evan Knott snorted and shook his head. "Like these situations ever go well."

Janet nodded. "Which is why we're here. Evan, Roger, get the trail packs ready. Be sure to set up packs for our people already in the field and don't forget the walkie talkies. Clara, Anita, notify your families. You'll be holding down the fort here until this is resolved. Questions?"

"What about the law enforcement rangers?" Deputy Roger Jepperson asked. "Are you calling them in? It's their territory."

Janet held up her cell phone. "I'll be contacting them while you guys get the packs ready."

Roger gave a curt nod. "If you have a choice, ask for Ranger Hank Lloyd. I've worked with him before. He's a great tracker and a good detective. Plus, he's got an easy-going personality."

"Good to know," Janet said. "I'll ask about him, but we'll work with whoever we can get."

An hour later, Janet had contacted the Beartooth Ranger District headquarters in Red Lodge, Montana. The head law enforcement ranger for the region had agreed to assign rangers to work with the Garnet County Sheriff's department if required. Since the rangers were an easy two-and-a-half hours away, he'd agreed to send an advance team to Billings where they would wait for Chief Deputy Millson's call to action.

Satisfied with the outcome, Janet turned her attention to inspecting the packs Evan and Roger had put together before checking in with Clara and Anita to make sure they were ready to handle the office during the team's absence.

With everything as organized as she could make it, she settled at her desk to deal with writing a report on the day's events. And to wait for Jason's call. Which she hoped would not include a request for back-up.

She looked up from her computer and reflected on the

outcome she'd like to see. That would be for Jason and his men to find the Richardson girl with as little trouble as possible.

That would be ideal.

She sighed and returned to her report. She'd been a deputy long enough to know that outcomes were rarely ideal. It paid to be prepared, and Janet and her team were as prepared as a county sheriff's department in rural Montana could be.

Now she just had to wait for the sheriff's next move.

8

LORI RICHARDSON

Darrin led Lori into their camp. It wasn't much to look at, but they did have a lean-to built from scrap lumber and branches covered with a worn tarp. There was a firepit dug out and lined with stones several feet from the lean-to and a make-shift larder hung from a sturdy tree branch even further from the lean-to. She noted they even had a privy of sorts set up, complete with a roll of toilet paper stuck on a handy branch and a garden trowel for burying the results.

She'd seen better camps, but she'd also seen worse. Much worse.

"Here we are," Darrin said as he untied the rope from her wrists. "Home sweet home."

Lori rubbed her chafed wrists as she gazed around, wondering if she could escape now that her hands were free.

"Don't even think about running," Bart said. "I'd hate to have to shoot you after we took the trouble to bring you home."

Ignoring Bart, she eyed Darrin. "What is it you expect me to do?"

"Well, right now how about you fix us a bite to eat?" He strode to a pile of branches and began breaking them into lengths that would fit in the firepit. "Bart, get the food down so Lori can see what she has to work with."

Bart grumbled but headed to the tree and lowered the burlap bag containing their larder to the ground. He beckoned to Lori.

"Come here, girlie," he called with a leering note in his voice. "I've got what you need right here." He cupped his crotch as he added that last.

Lori glanced at Darrin, but he was busy building the fire. She didn't want to approach Bart, but she didn't want to anger Darrin either. So far, he seemed to be the safer of the two.

"Bring the bag over here," she called. "Do you have a pan?"

Bart scowled, but picked up the burlap bag and dumped it at her feet before moving into the lean-to and emerging with a cast iron skillet.

Rummaging through the food bag, Lori found a few bruised apples, a slab of uncured bacon, and half a loaf of stale bread. Once she had the heavy skillet in her hands, she felt safer. Hot or cold, the cast iron utensil would make a fine weapon should she need one.

After finding a good-sized flat rock to act as a cutting board, she asked Darrin for a knife.

He looked at her through narrowed eyes. "What for?"

She gave an exasperated sigh. "You asked me to fix food. I need to cut strips off this bacon and slice the bread. The apples need to be cored." She stood and placed her hands on her hips. "Do you want me to do it, or do you want to? Either works for me."

He stared at her for another minute before nodding and handing her his hunting knife, hilt first. "Don't try anything."

"Wouldn't dream of it," she muttered. Slicing strips from the slab of bacon, she placed them in the pan then set the pan on the fire. "Got any plates?"

Bart ducked into the lean-to and returned with three tin pans and couple of forks.

Lori cut thick slices of stale bread while the bacon sizzled. Lifting the crisp bacon onto one of the plates, she dragged three slices of bread through the drippings then set the bread to fry while she trimmed the apples.

When all was ready, she returned the knife to Darrin, and the three of them settled to a quick meal of fried bread, bacon, and apple slices.

"Damn," Bart said, patting his stomach. "That's the best meal I've had in ages." He turned to Darrin and grinned. "Why didn't you find us a woman months ago?"

Darrin sopped the end of the bacon grease out of the skillet with the last bite of bread before popping it in his mouth. "Her cooking sure beats yours, Bart. That's a damn true fact."

Lori rolled her eyes and wondered what they'd been eating. She certainly hadn't cooked anything special. Her brothers would've thought the meal sub-par. Of course, her brothers would've made sure any camp of theirs had adequate supplies.

She was just lifting the skillet off the rock when she heard it. A sharp rustling in the undergrowth, followed by Charlie's voice yelling for her.

"Charlie!" she screamed, her heart thundering loudly enough she was sure he'd hear it. "I'm here! I'm here, Charlie!"

Darrin's hand clamped over her mouth, muffling any further screams. "You shut up," he growled, "unless you want *Charlie* to end up like that horse of yours."

Her stomach lurched with fear, but this was her chance. She swept the cast iron skillet up and over her shoulder, catching Darrin by surprise. He yelped, released her, and she ran straight for the bushes where the rustling noises had originated.

A shot rang out just as Darrin lunged for her, caught the back of her jeans and yanked her off her feet. The skillet flew out of her hand and she was dragged back from her hoped for escape route. Darrin pushed her against the far side of huge Ponderosa pine, yelling for Bart to kill the bastards. Then he whipped out a red checked bandana and gagged her.

Before she was even sure what had happened, Darrin was dragging her through the trees with Bart covering their retreat.

9

SHERIFF REYNOLDS

S heriff Jason Reynolds swore as he knelt beside Charlie Richardson and worked to stop the blood pouring from the gunshot wound in the young man's side.

"You young idiot," he snarled, accepting the fabric strips Ethan had torn from him own shirt. "If you'd stayed quiet and followed orders, Lori'd be safe and you wouldn't be gunshot." He turned to Ethan. "Are you steady enough to finish binding this?"

The older man nodded, though his face was nearly white with shock at seeing his younger son bleeding on the forest floor. He glanced at Jason as he took the fabric strips from him. "She answered Charlie." His eyes begged Jason for confirmation. "At least we know she's still alive."

Jason switched places with Ethan. "Yes. At least we know that."

He stood and stepped away, leaving Charlie's care to his father and older brother. Calling his deputies over, Jason said, "Eric, call Janet. Get emergency evac here for Charlie. Ask her to send back-up." He glanced at Adam and clapped him on the shoulder. "This is turning into quite the experience for your first field work with our department."

Adam glanced at Charlie and shrugged. "Now I know why you wanted to leave them behind."

"Indeed." Jason pulled his Stetson off and wiped the sweat from his brow with his sleeve. "Okay. Let's you and me take a look around and see if we can tell which direction they took off in. Go in quiet," he finished. "I don't think it's likely, but one of them might have stayed behind to try to pick us off one by one."

Adam nodded, his face grim, and the two of them moved quietly through the undergrowth toward where the shots had been fired. What they found was a deserted camp. The fire in the pit still burned and a heavy, cast iron skillet lay upended in the dirt.

Studying the scene, Jason commented, "This wasn't set up this morning. They'd been here a while."

Adam nodded, pointing out the food bag that Bart had returned to the tree while Lori was cooking. "They even had a larder of sorts." Pulling the bag down, he inspected the contents. "I wonder where they got the slab of bacon and the bread?"

Jason searched through the lean-to. "Some of this stuff they may have packed in, like the sleeping bags and pads, but I'm betting they've been raiding other folks' camps."

"Over here, Sheriff," Adam called. When Jason joined him, he pointed to the broken branches and disturbed undergrowth. "Looks like they headed off through the brush. Didn't bother with a game trail this time."

"That should be easy to follow."

"Yep," Adam agreed. "And it means they'll be slower than they were this morning. Breaking trail takes more effort than just hiking." He paused before adding, "Especially when one of your party is unwilling."

Jason grimaced. "I hope the girl isn't *too* uncooperative. I'd hate for them to decide she's too much trouble and just shoot her."

Adam swallowed hard, his Adam's apple bobbing. "I hadn't thought of that. Think it's a possibility?"

"Definitely. Especially if they think we're getting too close." Jason glanced back toward where the Richardsons waited for evacuation. "After all, they've already shot one man and for all they know, he's dead. A second body wouldn't be a problem to them. Not if they think killing her will give them a better chance of disappearing into the wilderness."

Adam shot a hot glance at their trail, before asking Jason, "What now? Do we follow or wait for back-up?"

Jason stared into the brush and ground his teeth in frustration. He wanted to follow, but he needed to make sure the Richardsons got away safely. Plus, he knew it would be smarter to wait for back-up. Shaking his head, he turned back toward where they'd left the others.

"We wait for back-up." He caught Adam's gaze and studied his new deputy. "Are you comfortable staking out this camp alone? I want to check on the others, but I want this camp covered in case they circle back."

Adam nodded. "I'm fine with that."

"You sure? You could go back while I wait. You could send Eric to me."

"No need," Adam said, shaking his head. "I'll be ready for them if they come back."

"Good enough." Jason turned and strode back the way they had come.

10

CHIEF DEPUTY JANET MILLSON

C hief Deputy Janet Millson studied the topo map while she listened to Deputy Eric Lawson's report over the phone. Her end was on speaker and the bull-pen was deathly quiet as the other members of the team listened in.

"Okay," she said. "So you've got one injured civilian in need of medical attention and the sheriff wants back-up. Where are you? Can you give me coordinates?"

"No problem. I grabbed our newest sat phone. It has built in GPS tracking. Just a sec while I access that information."

Once Janet had the coordinates, she contacted emergency services and requested a helicopter large enough to evacuate three men and carry in a back-up crew of law enforcement officers. Next, she contacted the rangers waiting in Billings and told them where to meet the helicopter.

Finally, she turned to her own deputies. "All right. Here's the plan. The helicopter will meet us as close to the coordinates Eric provided as possible. They'll ferry in the rangers and bring the Richardsons out. We'll drive out to the Richardson ranch, then take four wheelers out to the canyon where Jason and the others went in. We're in for a hike, so make sure you have plenty of water and energy bars in those packs.

She turned to Clara, who had been listening in. "Clara, you and Anita are in charge. Anything that comes up that you can't handle, call on Sheriff Porter over in Dawes County. I've already given him a heads up and he's willing to step in if needed."

Clara nodded. "We'll take care of everything."

Janet, Evan, and Roger were shouldering their packs when the front door opened and the sheriff's wife, Kristi Lundrigan Reynolds stepped in. An attractive woman, Kristi sported shoulder length blonde hair tied up in a high ponytail. Her blue eyes expressed her concern for the safety of her husband and his deputies. She carried a large paper bag with a *Roasted Beans* logo on the side.

Janet stifled a groan. She didn't have time to fill the sheriff's wife in on everything that had happened this morning.

"Sorry, Kristi," she said. "We're just heading out to help Jason and his team. Clara will have to fill you in."

"I understand," Kristi said quickly. "I just wanted to drop this off. Food for twelve. It's sandwiches, cookies, and apples. Easily packable."

Irritated at the delay, but recognizing that Jason and Eric and Adam had already been in the field since morning and without the proper equipment, Janet swung her pack off her shoulders and motioned for Evan and Roger to do the same.

They quickly distributed the rations between the packs, then settled them back on their shoulders.

"Thanks for thinking of us, Kristi. I'm sure Jason and the others will be grateful for something more palatable than just energy bars."

"No problem," Kristi replied. "I'm just glad I caught you."

"All right. We're out of here."

"Take care and bring everyone back safely," Kristi called as the deputies strode through the front door.

Turning to Clara, she said, "Okay, now that we're alone, tell me everything."

———

By the time Janet and her deputies caught up with the emergency services people she was tired of carrying not only her pack, but one for Jason as well. Each of the three had shouldered the necessity of two packs in order to make sure that the sheriff and his advance team were provisioned.

It had been an exhausting hike. But just ahead the well-worn path branched. She would've have wondered which direction to follow if it weren't for the EMT sitting on a fallen log waiting for them. He stood as they approached.

"You must be Chief Deputy Millson," he said, holding out his hand. "I'm Lieutenant Steven Jeffers. Emergency services decided you folks could use a paramedic on this manhunt. Just in case. Sheriff Reynolds asked me to wait here and guide you the rest of the way in."

Janet shook the man's hand, then she, Evan, and Roger lowered their packs, pulled out canteens and drank before dropping to sit on the ground.

Finally, she said, "Yes, I'm Janet Millson. Glad to meet you, Lt. Jeffers. I sure hope we won't need your services, but glad to have you along. Did the rangers arrive in time to hitch a ride? Did your people get the Richardsons out?"

Jeffers nodded. "Yes to both questions. You'll meet the rangers when we get to the campsite. Charlie Richardson was placed on a backboard and carried to the helicopter. His father and brother accompanied him."

"What was his condition?" Janet asked.

"He was stable, but still had a bullet in his side." Jeffers paused before adding, "Your sheriff did a good job getting the bleeding under control, but it's good that we got here as soon as we did."

Janet jerked her chin toward the other trail. "I take it that's the path to where the helicopter landed?"

"It is. And when you're ready, I'll take you to the sheriff. He'll be glad to see you... and the supplies you've carried in."

Janet stood, her deputies following suit. As they gathered up all the packs, she said, "We're ready. Let's get this done."

11

SHERIFF REYNOLDS

A surge of relief swept through Jason when Janet, Evan, and Roger followed the paramedic into the kidnappers' camp. Finally. He had his own team all together again. He was glad to have help from the law enforcement rangers, and the paramedic was an excellent addition, but his own people! Deputies he knew and whose abilities he trusted... their presence was a definite relief. He'd already had one man injured on this manhunt; he didn't want another. And having his own team— people who were accustomed to his thought processes and to obeying his orders— lessened that possibility.

"Glad to see you found us," he said to Janet as she strode into the camp. He nodded to Jeffers. "Thanks for waiting for them."

"No problem, sir. We're all on the same team."

"Speaking of teams," Janet said, "we brought supplies for you three since you weren't expecting a wilderness adventure when you left the office this morning." With that, she and Roger and Evan handed their extra packs to Jason, Adam, and Eric.

"Awesome," Eric exclaimed. "Got any food or water in these?"

Evan nodded and managed to keep a straight face. "Sure. Energy bars."

Eric's face fell before he even opened his pack.

"Oh, come on," Roger said to Evan. "Play nice."

Janet shook her head. "Boys! Jason, Kristi stopped by just as we were leaving. There are enough sandwiches, cookies, and apples in the packs for all of us." She nodded to the rangers and the paramedic. "You guys too."

One of the rangers held up his hands. "Count us out. We just arrived and all of us have eaten already."

"Great," said Adam. "More for us! And we're starving."

Jason pulled out a sandwich and unwrapped it. He smiled. Ham and cheese. His favorite! "Pace yourselves, guys. We may want to divvy the rest of these out later."

Janet sat down on one of the logs that had been arranged around the now cold firepit. "In the spirit of team building, why don't we introduce ourselves. I'm Chief Deputy Janet Millson. Janet will do for the duration."

"Lt. Steven Jeffers, paramedic. Please, call me Steve."

"Law Enforcement Ranger Liam Baines," said a tall, blonde man, mid-thirties, wearing a ranger uniform of dark green trousers and light green, short-sleeved, button front shirt. With his matching ball cap, backpack, and rugged hiking boots, he looked completely ready for the trail. "Forget the title. Name's Liam."

The next guy, also in ranger uniform but with coal black hair and built like a wrestler, said, "Same designation as Liam. I'm Henry Lloyd. Call me Hank."

The third and final ranger stepped forward. Taller than Liam, this man was whip thin. With graying sandy hair and pronounced facial lines, he seemed older than the other two. "Same title, though I'm the team leader. Elijah Kendrick. I go by Eli."

"Good to meet you all," Janet said with a nod. "We're happy to have your help." Pointing to the two deputies she'd brought along, who were busy devouring their food, she introduced them.

"The tall, skinny guy over there is Deputy Evan Knott." Evan raised a hand. "The redhead next to him is Deputy Roger Jepperson." After Roger waved at everyone, Janet continued, "We're pretty informal. First names will do."

"That includes me," said Jason, wiping his fingers on the napkin his wife had provided. "No need to stand on ceremony."

Rising to his feet, he nodded to the older ranger. "Eli, I think we're ready to take a look at that map you brought." Turning to Janet, he explained, "I wanted to wait until you got here before we talked strategy."

After a few minutes of studying the topographical map a decision was made. As long as the kidnappers' trail was easy to distinguish, they'd move forward as a group. If and when their prey managed to hide their tracks, they'd separate into three or four groups, each with at least one deputy and one ranger. The paramedic would stay with Jason's group.

Plan in mind, the manhunt began in earnest.

KRISTI LUNDRIGAN REYNOLDS

Having gotten all the latest news from Clara, Kristi returned to *Delectable Mountain Quilting*, her quilt shop and official home-away-from-home. The moment she stepped through the door the familiar, comforting scents of quilting cottons, fabric dyes, and herbal tea surrounded her. As did her employees!

"What did you find out?" asked Mattie Stebbings, Kristi's chief clerk and former owner of the shop.

"Is Lori okay?" Andrea Jansson asked. Andrea, a part-time employee, was also a student at the same college Lori attended in Billings. They weren't in the same year, but as residents of the same small community, they knew each other fairly well. Plus, Kristi knew that Andrea had a crush on Charlie, the younger of Lori's two older brothers.

Kristi took Andrea's hands and squeezed. "They haven't rescued Lori yet, but Jason won't stop until she's home." Gesturing to the overstuffed chair near the front window, Kristi said, "Since we don't have any customers, let's sit down. Andrea, you take the big chair, Mattie and I will grab folding chairs."

When they were all seated, Kristi leaned forward and told

them what Clara had passed along to her. "So you see," she finished, "the manhunt is really just getting started, but there's already been an injury, and I know that's only strengthened Jason's resolve."

"But what about Charlie?" Andrea asked, her voice breaking with fear. "Is he going to be all right?"

Kristi glanced at her friend and employee and then looked away. She knew how Andrea felt about the young man and could empathize with the younger woman's fear for his health and safety.

"I don't know, Andrea. I just know he's being air-lifted out by emergency services. I don't even know if they'll take him to Billings or bring him here to Garnet County Hospital."

Mattie reached out and patted Andrea's knee. "I'm sure he'll be fine, and even if they take him to Billings, his dad will bring him back here as soon as it's safe for him to travel."

Andrea swallowed and raised her chin. "You're right, of course. If he were seriously wounded, Clara would know."

Kristi nodded. "Clara knows everything," she said with a little laugh. "I sometimes wonder if she's psychic."

"Right?" agreed Mattie. "If anything terrible happens, Clara will let Kristi know… and then we'll know."

"Definitely," Kristi said.

Just then the doorbell jingled and Mattie rose to meet the customer.

Kristi patted Andrea's hand. "Are you all right, or do you need to head home?"

Andrea managed a small smile. "I'm fine, just worried. I won't be any less worried at home, and here I have work to keep my mind busy."

"I know what you mean." Kristi rose, folded up the chairs she and Mattie had been using and moved to put them away while Andrea went to the cutting table to finish cutting and folding fat quarters for display.

Later that afternoon, Kristi called Clara to see if there was any news.

"Not from the search," Clara said, "but the Richardson men are back in Garnet Gateway at the hospital. Charlie is doing well and the Billings doctor gave them permission to transfer him here."

"Oh! That is good news. Thank you, Clara." Kristi paused before ending the call, and then asked, "Do you think it would be all right if I went by to see them? I don't want to intrude."

"Oh, Kristi, I think that would be lovely. I'm sure Ethan and Luke would appreciate knowing you're concerned. And, in a way, you represent the department, being the sheriff's wife and all."

"That's a good thought. Thanks again, Clara."

"Not at all. That's what I'm here for."

Once she ended the call, Kristi went to find Andrea.

"Charlie is here in our hospital," she said. "I'm going to go check on him and see if Ethan or Luke need anything." She paused, smiled, and asked, "Want to come along?"

Andrea's face lit up, her eyes sparkling. "Really?"

"Really. We're not all that busy. I'm sure Mattie can hold down the fort. Grab your things while I let Mattie know what we're up to."

"Thank you, Kristi! This means the world to me."

13

BART BLAKESLEY

B art was mad. He and Darrin had done it. They'd found themselves a woman, but just as they settled into camp with a good meal in their bellies, they'd been forced to run from their comfortable home... and before he'd gotten a taste of that pretty little female currently sashaying in front of him.

Damn their luck! He should be back in camp humping that enticing gal right now. His eyes slid out of focus as he imagined stroking her soft skin and tasting her sweet honey, but no! He was tramping through the undergrowth behind her while trying to keep his mind on listening to make sure they weren't being followed. He was tired of hiking. He wanted a nap. Preferably with her naked and tucked right in beneath him.

He shook his head to clear his thoughts and noticed her reel sideways, as if off balance. Narrowing his gaze, he saw it—the damn bitch was marking their trail!

Grabbing her arm, he barked at his partner. "Darrin! She's marking a path for them to follow."

Darrin stopped, turned, and studied the broken twig Bart pointed to, then he studied Lori. He slapped her, open-handed, but hard enough to leave a significant red imprint.

Turning to Bart, he said, "Doesn't matter. We're leaving enough sign a blind man could follow. There's a stream just ahead. When we get there, we'll walk through the water for a while. Throw them off our scent."

Lori covered the imprint of Darrin's hand with her own, as if protecting her injured cheek. He'd hit close enough to her eye that it was swollen. That didn't stop her from glaring at the men.

"Where are you taking me now?" she asked, her voice sullen.

"To our second camp." Darrin grinned at her. "What? You didn't think we were smart enough to plan ahead?" He shook his head. "You're ours now, little lady, and we'll shoot anyone who tries to take you back." He paused before adding, "Just like we did that last guy. What was it you called him? Charlie? Doubt he'll be chasing us any further."

Tears welled in Lori's eyes, but she refused to let them fall. Instead, she raised her chin and looked away.

Bart smiled. He liked the way her eyes glittered when they were filled with tears. He'd have to make sure that happened often. When Darrin turned back to the trail, Bart gave her a push to get her started walking again.

"No more *stumbling* into bushes and breaking twigs," he growled. "Learn to hike carefully or I'll sling you over my shoulder and carry you to our other camp."

He was quiet for a moment before he sidled up close to her and spoke directly into her ear. "Come to think of it, I'd like to have you hanging over my shoulder. Go ahead. Break some more twigs."

She shoulder butted him, and he grinned. Sure was gonna be fun breaking her in!

After another half-hour or so of walking, Bart heard water rushing ahead. A few minutes later they came in sight of a good-sized stream. Pushing Lori to sit on the sandy dirt of the bank, he plopped down beside her. Darrin dropped to the ground on her other side.

They still hadn't heard any sound of pursuit. Either the lawmen were better woodsmen than they expected or they weren't anywhere close.

"Take off your boots and socks, Bart," Darrin said, "and roll up your pants as far as you can." He started the same process himself. "We'll tie our laces together and hang our boots over our shoulders while we wade through the water."

Bart nodded. "Got it." He noticed Lori wasn't moving. She wasn't prepping for their walk in the water. He glanced at Darrin, caught his gaze, and nodded to Lori's feet. Darrin just shrugged.

"You willing to carry her?"

Bart leered. "You bet. Been waiting all day to get my hands on that firm body."

Lori's face paled and she started unlacing her boots.

Darrin laughed. "Thought that would get you moving!"

Bart's face darkened and he yanked the knot of his laces tight. The thought of carrying the pretty little gal had excited him. Now he wouldn't get to. His eyes lit with an idea. Maybe he'd make sure she fell in the stream… then she'd have to strip so her clothes could dry. His mouth watered as he let his gaze roam over her. He'd sure like to see what was hiding under that plaid shirt and blue jeans.

Lori looked up and caught him staring at her. "What? I'm doing what Darrin asked."

Bart licked his lips. "Yeah, but I'd rather you didn't."

She turned away, stood, and settled the tied laces of her hiking boots over her shoulder and stuffed her socks in the front pockets of her jeans.

He thought he heard her whisper, "Tough nuts." He grinned. He couldn't wait to have her naked body writhing beneath him. He'd show her just how tough his nuts were… and she'd beg for more!

14

SHERIFF REYNOLDS

J ason and Eli hunkered down beside Adam on the bank of a slow-moving stream. Adam pointed out depressions in the sandy soil.

"See? They settled here, all three of them." He glanced back the way they'd come. "They were all wearing boots until they got here." He pointed to a couple of marks leading to the water. "They're barefoot there."

Jason nodded. "Makes sense. They wouldn't want to tramp around in wet boots if they could avoid it." He glanced at Eli. "Any idea where they're headed?"

Eli stood and stared around. "Not really, though there are plenty of caves up ahead in those rocky hills. If they're headed to one of those, we should see their trail start to climb soon."

"I'd sure like to catch them before we lose their trail in those rocks." Jason straightened and brushed dirt from his jeans. "Adam, why don't you cross the stream and find where they left the water. The rest of us will refill our canteens and get ready to follow when you give the word."

"On it," Adam said and dropped to the sandy dirt to remove his boots and socks.

"All right, everyone," Jason called. "Looks like we'll be doing some wading, so get ready. Be sure to refill your canteens since we don't know where our next water source will be."

"I've got iodine tablets, if anyone needs them," Steve, their paramedic, added.

As everyone settled to their tasks, Jason and Eli dropped to the ground and pulled their packs from their shoulders. Both riffled through their belongings and came up with energy bars. Glancing at each other, they laughed.

"Great minds," Jason said and toasted Eli with his bar.

"Might as well have a snack while we wait for your deputy to point us in the right direction," Eli said.

They glanced around and saw that the other members of their team had taken their cue from them. Everyone was either drinking from a canteen or chewing on an energy bar.

"We've got good people with good instincts," Jason said after swallowing a bite. "Don't need to be told to hydrate and eat."

"Yep," agreed Eli. "They all know what they're about."

Just then Adam waded out of the stream and dropped to the ground next to them.

"There's no sign that they left the water anywhere near here."

Jason frowned. "You sure? They didn't just make an effort to cover their tracks?"

Adam pulled an energy bar from his pack, uncapped his canteen and took a swig, then bit into the bar. He swallowed, then nodded and said, "I'm sure."

"Damn," Eli swore. "I was hoping they were stupid."

Jason nodded. "Well, no help for it. We'll have to split up and search the far bank." He studied Adam as the man ate. "What do you think? Search from the water, or cross the stream and search on land?"

Adam frowned. "Hard to say. We're less likely to corrupt the trail from the water—no one will walk over their tracks without noticing, but we're more likely to miss their exit completely if we're in the water—especially folks who aren't accustomed to tracking."

Eli nodded. "It's a toss-up." He glanced at Jason. "Your call, Sheriff."

Jason stood and paced around the camp, considering his options. When he reached his decision, he moved to the center of the group and stood with fists on hips.

"Okay, here's what's happening. Since Adam didn't find their exit point, we're going to break into teams. Some of us will search for their trail from the water, some from the ground."

He met the gaze of each member of his team in turn. Nine of the best folks he'd ever worked with. Ten counting himself. They could do this. They'd find Lori Richardson and lock her abductors away for as long as the law would allow.

"Eli, who's your best tracker?"

Eli studied the other two rangers a moment, then said, "Hank."

Liam nodded.

"Great," Jason said. "Hank, you and Janet will stick to the water and head downstream, watching for their exit point."

Janet and Hank exchanged a glance, nodded to each other, then said in unison, "Yes, sir."

Jason continued, "Adam and Eli, head upstream but search from the water. The rest of us will cover the ground. Those of us on land will have to be extra vigilant to ensure that we don't stomp right over their trail."

He took a deep breath and wiped the sweat from his forehead before finishing the assignments. "Eric, Roger, and Liam, you'll head upstream. Evan and Steve, you'll come with me downstream."

The group broke into their teams and finished prepping for the next phase of the search. When canteens were all filled and everyone had boots dangling from their shoulders, Jason called for attention.

"All right. You all know your assignments. Let's move out. Keep your walkie talkies ready and let the rest of us know as soon as you find their trail. Let's go bring Lori home!"

15

KRISTI LUNDRIGAN REYNOLDS

As Kristi and Andrea walked into Garnet County Hospital, Kristi reflected on how lucky their small community was to have this resource. It was only a 25-bed facility, but it was fully accredited and offered several departments including a birth center, general surgery, radiology, and emergency medicine 24 hours a day, seven days a week. Not every community the size of Garnet Gateway had access to such great services.

The women entered through the sliding glass doors and headed straight for the reception desk.

"Good afternoon," the young woman manning the desk said. "How can we help you today?"

Kristi smiled, and reading the woman's name tag, said, "Good afternoon, Jenny. We're here to check on Charlie Richardson. I believe he was transferred in from Billings earlier today. Is he able to have visitors?"

"Let me check," Jenny said, turning to her computer. After a few moments of clicking her keyboard and studying the screen, she smiled. "He's in room 124. Just down that hallway," she said, motioning them in the proper direction.

"Thank you," Kristi said as she and Andrea turned to the hallway.

Before they reached Charlie's room, they spotted Ethan Richardson leaning against a wall, head tilted back and eyes closed.

"Mr. Richardson?" Andrea said, obviously alarmed. "Is everything all right?"

Ethan straightened away from the wall and focused on the young woman.

"Andrea? Andrea Jansson?" he asked, blinking several times as if to clear his vision. "What are you doing here?"

Andrea lowered her eyes, blushing, so Kristi stepped in.

"Mr. Richardson, I'm Kristi Reynolds. Sheriff Reynolds' wife. Clara Dahl, the dispatcher for the sheriff's department, let me know that Charlie had been transferred here. I came to check on him and since Andrea is a friend, she came with me."

Ethan scrubbed his face with both hands before nodding and glancing at Andrea. "I see," he said. "Forgive me. It's been a very long day and I'm not at my best."

"Understood," Kristi said. "How is Charlie?"

He smiled grimly. "He's doing fine for a boy with a gunshot wound. I'm sorry," he said, shaking his head. "Andrea, why don't you go in and say hello. I'm sure Charlie will be glad to see you. Luke is with him so you won't have to do anything for him."

As Andrea opened the door and stepped inside, Ethan gestured Kristi across the hall. "There's a waiting room over there. Why don't we sit down and talk for a minute."

Kristi followed Ethan into a sunny room with several comfortable-looking chairs, a small television, two end tables piled with magazines, and a wall of windows providing a view of the 'Sorkees. As soon as they were seated, Ethan asked, "Do you have any news? Any word on the search for my Lori?"

Sadly, Kristi shook her head. "You probably know as much as

I do. I stopped by the station to deliver some food for the searchers and caught Janet Millson and the rest of the deputies just as they were leaving to join the search. I haven't heard anything since, except when Clara called to let me know you and your sons were here."

Ethan leaned forward, elbows on knees, head in hands. "This has been the worst day of my life. Lori kidnapped. Charlie shot. Lori's mare killed." He raised his head and met her gaze. "What if they don't find her? What if Lori is gone forever?"

"Don't say that, Mr. Richardson." Kristi reached out and touched his arm briefly. "Don't even think it."

"Ethan," he said with a tight smile. "Call me Ethan."

She nodded. "And you should call me Kristi." After a moment's pause, she continued, "Ethan, my husband is very good at his job. He'll find Lori and he'll bring her abductors to justice."

"I know he'll try, but the 'Sorkees cover a lot of area, and he's just one man."

"One man backed up by five dedicated—and very capable—deputies. Plus he has several law enforcement rangers helping. Those men and women know what they're doing. They'll find Lori and bring her home."

He sighed. "I sure hope you're right."

Kristi nodded emphatically. "I am. You can count on it. Now, what do you and your sons need? Will you and Luke be going back to the ranch, or are you staying in town to be close to Charlie?"

Before Kristi and Andrea left they'd arranged a food train for Ethan and Luke—lunches to be delivered to the hospital, dinners to the Garnet Gateway Inn where Kristi had arranged for them to have a room at a substantially reduced fee. Garnet Gateway folks pulled together when there was need.

Once Charlie was released to go home, Andrea would see to it that meals were delivered daily for at least a week. Likely longer.

In the meantime, Ethan had talked to his head ranch hand who would see to the running of the ranch in the Richardsons' absence.

Life went on for the Richardson family, but it would go on a lot better once Lori came home.

16

SHERIFF REYNOLDS

Once the land teams were across the stream, Jason watched as his water teams headed away from each other. Both pairs hugged the shore, studying the bank as they waded through the slow-moving stream.

He joined the rest of the land teams, sitting on the sandy bank, drying his feet, and getting his socks and boots back on. When everyone was ready, the upstream team headed out with Eric in the lead.

Jason glanced at Evan and Steve. "Leave your packs here for the moment. Let's take a closer look at the area and make sure they didn't cover their tracks at the stream and fool us into thinking they came out somewhere else."

They scoured the area, but didn't find any sign of the men they were hunting. Nor did they find any of the broken twigs that Lori had been leaving to guide them.

Finally, Jason gave up. "Okay," he said, picking up his pack and slinging it over his shoulder. "Adam was right. They didn't come out here." He watched as Evan and Steve shouldered their gear. "Let's move out. Step carefully and watch for any sign."

They moved in a rough line. Jason walked right next to the

stream with Steve a few feet further into the scrub brush and Evan a little further still. Each man moved slowly and carefully, studying the ground and the undergrowth. It was tedious, but they felt sure they weren't missing any sign of human passage.

Jason hoped one of the other teams was having better luck, but his walkie talkie didn't squawk. No one had found any sign yet.

After a frustrating hour, Jason motioned for Evan and Steve to join him. They sat on the stream bank and drank from their canteens, while Jason checked in with the other teams.

"This is Sheriff Reynolds," he said into the crackling walkie talkie. "What's your status?"

Janet responded first. "We're still in the water, though my feet have gone numb. No sign yet."

Jason smiled grimly. "Sorry about the numb feet. No sign from us either."

"Nothing from us either," Adam reported. "And our feet are numb too."

"Our feet are fine," Eric said, and Jason could almost see his grin, "but no sign of a trail yet."

"Okay, everyone," Jason said. "Take a break. Hydrate. Water teams, beach yourselves and dry your feet. We'll start again in fifteen."

The other teams acknowledged his instructions and the walkie talkies fell silent. Jason leaned back on his elbows and studied the sky. Mid-afternoon. He'd hoped to have Lori safe and be on the way back to the Richardson ranch by now. But he'd been a lawman long enough to know things rarely went as easily as he hoped.

He thought about Kristi and smiled. His wife was rarely far from his thoughts. The last six months had been the best of his life. They'd married last Thanksgiving—for the second time.

He shook his head. He still couldn't believe he'd been stupid enough to lose her the first time around. His one night stand with a call girl during that convention in Denver had been... interesting. But it sure hadn't been worth the price he'd paid: Kristi's trust and, ultimately, his marriage. He sure as hell wouldn't make that mistake again.

Kristi was the love of his life and he was damn lucky she'd given him a second chance... even if it had taken him nearly two-and-a-half years to earn her trust once more. And get her to marry him. Again.

He'd already known she was the only woman for him and that he needed her in his life. The problem? He hadn't been at all sure that she needed him. Even if she did still love him—and he'd thought she did—she'd proven that she could live just fine without him.

She'd taken the inheritance her grandmother had left her and bought a quilt shop, which she'd built into a thriving business. She was financially secure with loyal employees who were also her friends and a whole community of local women, quilters as well as others, who thought the world of her.

What did she need him for?

Luckily, she loved Jason just as much as he loved her. So, when he finally worked up the nerve to ask, she agreed to marry him. Again.

He was the luckiest man in the world!

Now, he just needed that luck to help him find Lori and take her home to her father and brothers. Hopefully whole and unharmed.

With that in mind, he stood, shouldered his pack, and said, "Break's over. Let's get moving."

17

CHIEF DEPUTY JANET MILLSON

C hief Deputy Janet Millson was severely tired of wading in this cold mountain stream. The word *cold* had taken on new meaning for her. Her feet were so numb she couldn't even feel them! Most folks would think that was a good thing; if she couldn't feel her feet, she wouldn't feel the cold.

Most people would be wrong.

The cold radiated up her legs, making her blood feel sluggish. And for another treat, the numbness made walking in the stream more difficult—she couldn't feel the rocks that wanted to slide beneath her. She was lucky she hadn't twisted an ankle or dumped her whole body in that icy water.

She kept her complaints to herself though. Her partner, Law Enforcement Ranger Hank Lloyd hadn't made so much as a peep about the cold or his own discomfort. No way would she be the first to say anything. She wouldn't allow him to think she was a wimp. So she sucked up her discomfort and clenched her teeth to keep them from chattering.

Suddenly, Hank stopped, then stepped carefully from the water and bent to examine the sandy dirt on the shore.

"Find something?" Janet asked, wading closer to him.

He nodded. "They left the water here. Take a look."

Hank moved sideways a couple of feet to give her room to stand. Janet stepped gratefully out of the icy stream and hunkered down to check Hank's find.

Glancing up at him, she said, "You're right. Those are definitely human prints and they're fresh, but I don't know how you spotted them from the water."

He grinned. "Years of experience. Let's settle over there, away from their trail, dry our feet and get our boots back on. We should probably let the Sheriff know what we found."

"Great," Janet agreed, sitting where he'd indicated and rubbing her cold feet. "I'll make the call right now." Pulling her boots away from where they'd been dangling by their laces over her shoulder, she shrugged out of her pack, and unclipped her walkie talkie from her belt.

"Sheriff Reynolds, this is Millson," she said into the two way radio. "Come in, Jason."

"Reynolds here," Jason said. "Go ahead, Janet."

"We've found their trail. Call the other teams in and meet us as soon as possible." She read their location coordinates from the walkie talkie screen and said, "Millson out."

"Great job, you two," Jason said. "We're on our way."

As soon as the other teams acknowledged the new direction, Janet clicked her radio off and set to brushing off her feet and putting her socks and boots back on.

Dry feet and warm socks! Heaven!

Weapons were the last thing on her mind when two men exploded out of the undergrowth, shot Hank, and pointed the barrel of a rifle at her heart.

"Give me that pistol you're packing. Nice and easy now. Don't make me nervous. I might shoot you by accident," said the taller of the two. His scruffy beard was streaked with gray and his blue eyes were as cold as the water Janet had just left. He jerked his head toward his partner as Janet tossed her gun in the dirt. "Check her pack. Make sure she doesn't have a second pistol."

"You're Darrin Haskin," she said. Watching the other man paw through her pack, she added, "And you're Bart Blakesley."

Bart's eyes jerked to Darrin, then focused on Janet. "How do you know our names?" He was obviously the muscle of the team, not the brains. Tall, thick set with almost no neck, his beard was a reddish hue and his gray-green eyes held a mean expression. He was built like a professional wrestler. A *big* wrestler with a vicious streak.

"Shut up!" Darrin growled. "You just told her she was right!" Turning his attention back to Janet, he said, "You're coming with us."

Janet glanced at Hank. The ranger was unconscious on the ground a few feet away. Blood seeped through his shirt, but at least it wasn't flowing fast... and Jason and the paramedic were headed their way. She hoped Hank would be okay.

She turned her attention to their attackers and shrugged. "I didn't need confirmation. I've seen wanted posters on both of you." She calmly finished tying her boot laces. "As for me going with you, if you'd waited a bit longer, I'd've come to you... along with several other lawmen." She glanced up at Darrin. "Where's Lori Richardson?"

Darrin leered at her. "Come along nice now and you'll find out."

Hank's eyes opened to a slit and he gave Janet a barely perceptible nod. He'd heard and would report to Jason and the others.

She just needed to buy him some time. She'd've liked to buy enough for the others to arrive before Darrin and Bart took her, but Bart was studying Hank, his big fingers playing around the rifle's trigger. She couldn't let the big man finish the ranger off.

Janet stood up so suddenly both perps focused on her, and only her.

"Well, all right then," she said loudly. "Take me to Lori. I need to make sure she's okay."

Darrin laughed. "Give us any trouble and Lori will need to make sure *you're* okay." He gestured to Bart. "Leave him. You take the lead this time. I'll watch the woman."

Bart snickered. "Of course you will. Now we each have a woman. This one's yours. I want Lori."

Janet glared at him. "I'm not a side of beef. Neither is Lori."

"No," Darrin agreed, his gaze roaming over her body. "You're a lot better. More useful too. Lori can cook. Bet you can hunt… if we ever trust you with a gun again."

"I can handle myself in the field," she said as she followed Bart away from the stream… and Hank. Too bad she hadn't had a chance to handle these scruffy men. But then that was the point of an ambush… to not give your opponent the opportunity to fight back.

18

SHERIFF REYNOLDS

Sheriff Jason Reynolds stormed through the thick undergrowth along the edge of the stream. Paramedic Steve Jeffers followed a few steps behind, managing not to get switched in the face as the ninebark and fool's huckleberry boughs snapped back into place after Jason pushed them aside. Deputy Evan Knott brought up the rear of their little train.

Jason had just punched through a particularly dense patch of bushes when he spotted Hank Lloyd lying unnaturally still on a clear space of the stream bank. Janet was nowhere in sight.

Rushing to Hank's side, Jason called over his shoulder, "Steve! Hank's been injured. Hurry!"

Steve rushed up, pulling his medical pack from his shoulder and kneeling to examine the ranger. "He's been shot," he said, "low on the left shoulder. Wound looks similar to Charlie Richardson's. Just guessing, but I'd say the bullet came from the same rifle."

Evan joined them and glanced around the small clearing. "Where's Janet?"

"I don't know," Jason replied. "Definitely not here. If Steve can bring him around, maybe Hank can tell us."

Steve probed the ranger's wound, raised his shoulder to check his back, and said, "He's lucky. It's a through-and-through and the shooter missed his heart by several inches. I'll clean the wound, bandage it, and he should be able to continue. It'll hurt like the devil, but only muscle tissue is involved, and I've got pain meds with me. We should be able to manage without having to airlift him out."

"That's good news," Jason said, relief washing over him. When he'd first seen Hank, he'd worried that the man was dead. "I'll let the others know what's happened." He paused and caught Steve's gaze. "The moment he comes to, ask him about Janet. Don't wait for me."

Steve nodded and went back to work on Hank's shoulder. "Will do."

"Evan, look around. See if you can find that bullet."

Jason pulled his walkie talkie from his belt and walked a few paces away to contact the other two search teams.

"We're close to your coordinates," Adam said, his voice sounding tinny over the radio. "Watching the stream bank, I'd say we're having an easier time getting to you than Eric and his team are. The undergrowth on the bank is pretty dense."

"It is," Eric agreed, "but we're making good time. We've been over this area once, so we're backtracking our own trail. Once we get to where we left the sheriff we should be able to follow his team's trail."

Jason nodded despite knowing none of them could see him. "Faster than breaking new trail, that's for sure. Hopefully, by the time all of you get here, Hank will be in good enough condition to continue. I have the feeling we're not far from where they've holed up. Reynolds out."

He clicked the radio off and clipped it back to his belt, turned, and strode back to Steve and Hank. Evan joined them a moment later, holding a small plastic vial. "Found the bullet," he said. "It's got a bit of fresh blood on it. No one will be able to claim it's been here for years."

"Excellent," Jason said, accepting the vial and stowing it in his pack. "We're going to put these guys away for a long time." He turned to Steve. "How's he doing?"

Hank's eyes fluttered open and he gave a grim smile. "Better than I was, thanks to you guys."

"Glad to hear it," Jason said, lowering himself to sit beside the injured man. "If you're up to it, tell us what happened."

"Let me get some water down him before he tries to talk," Steve said. He grabbed a canteen from his pack, put a hand behind Hank's head for support, lifted, and put the canteen to his patient's lips. After a moment he pulled it away. "Not too much too fast." He studied Hank's face. "I gave you a shot of antibiotics and as well as a pain killer. You should start to feel the effects soon."

Hank closed his eyes as Steve lowered his head back to the ground. "I'm feeling it already. Thanks, Doc."

Jason was antsy for news of Janet, but he waited as patiently as he could for Hank to recover from the effort of drinking a little water. Would the man be able to continue, if taking a drink took that much out of him? Or would Jason be forced to leave both him and Steve here beside the stream while the rest of them continued the search? He shook his head to dislodge the thought. Time would give him the answer; no need to worry about it in advance.

"Sheriff," Hank said. "I think I'm ready."

Jason nodded. "Let's hear it."

Hank licked his lips, then said, "I spotted this break in the undergrowth and moved closer to see if they might have left the water here. I found their tracks, and the place where they sat to get their boots back on. Three people. The lightest sat between the other two."

DEBBIE MUMFORD

"That's good," Evan said. "Lori's still with them and able to sit up."

Hank nodded. "Janet and I were hunkered down, getting our boots on when they attacked us. One of them shot me and the other one had Janet in his sights. There wasn't anything she could do."

"Was Lori with them?" Jason asked.

"Not that I saw."

"What happened to Janet?"

Hank closed his eyes and swallowed hard. "They took her. They were bragging about how they each had a woman now. The one who shot me was claiming Lori, telling the other guy he could have Janet."

Jason jumped to his feet, paced away and back again, cursing the whole time. Once he settled, Hank continued.

"I've got to give her credit. Janet was as calm as unruffled water. She back-talked them. Told them she would've come to them if they'd just waited. She also named them. Said she'd seen wanted posters for both."

"She recognized them?" Evan asked.

Hank nodded.

"Do you remember the names?" Jason asked.

"Darrin Haskin and Bart something," Hank answered. "I think it started with a 'B'... maybe Black or something."

"Blakesley," Evan said. "Darrin Haskin and Bart Blakesley." He turned to Jason. "I remember seeing that poster too. Janet and I were talking about them being wanted in Idaho and Wyoming as well as Montana. Bad dudes."

Hank struggled to sit upright, and Steve moved to help him. "Thanks. That pain killer is definitely working."

"Here," Steve said, pulling a sling and swathe unit from his pack. "Let's get that arm immobilized. Don't want your shoulder doing any work."

Jason paced around the clearing. "Okay. We know who we're

72

after and we know at least some of their intentions. They're looking for mates of a sort. Now they've got two."

"The good news," Hank said, "is that one of them is Janet. That woman is no pushover."

Jason nodded. "She's a fighter, and she knows what she's doing. She'll protect Lori. But we've got to find them and support her." He glanced at Hank. "Do you think you'll be able to go on, once the others get here?"

Hank grimaced, but nodded. "I will. I'm not leaving her in their hands. Either of them, but definitely not Janet."

The others nodded their agreement.

Darrin and Bart had made a huge mistake in taking Janet. On several levels.

19

CHIEF DEPUTY JANET MILLSON

J anet followed Bart Blakesley through the pine forest to the edge of a subalpine hillside. The new terrain was rocky, dotted with huge boulders, and sprinkled with bear-grass, thistle, and tall bluebells. The wildflowers were still in full bloom at this higher elevation and the hillside made a pretty picture in the late afternoon sunlight.

Studying the slope before her, Janet thought she spied a cave. Perhaps their destination? If so, it would be easy for the search party to overlook. The opening was low and surrounded by boulders. From some angles it would likely be invisible.

Darrin stepped up behind her and gave her a nudge forward. She'd stood still too long while studying the terrain.

"Like what you see?" he asked quietly.

"The wildflowers are pretty," she answered without so much as glancing at him. She'd have to make sure she marked their trail up this slope. She smiled. She'd insist on gathering a bouquet as they made their way up the slope. Maybe pull a few bluebells up by the roots, snap off the stem and leave the roots where they'd be noticed.

Yes. She had a plan.

Darrin objected when she picked the first plume of bear-grass, but relented when she pointed out that they'd left Lori alone all this time—probably tied up!—the young woman deserved something pretty to make up for the neglect.

By the time Janet paused beside a thistle bloom, Bart was on board enough with the idea to pull out a small folding knife and cut the prickly stem for Janet.

"Wouldn't want you to hurt yourself, now would we?" he asked with a smirk.

"Thanks," she said, accepting the thistle. "I hope wherever we're going isn't too far. I wouldn't want these to wilt before we get there."

"We're close," Darrin said, glancing over his shoulder toward the pine forest behind them. "You've got enough flowers. Let's get inside."

"Inside?" Janet asked looking around, her eyes wide. As if she hadn't noticed the cave even before they started across the open hillside.

Bart nodded to the low cave entrance. "Right there. You'll need to bend over to get inside, but there's room to stand once you're in."

"You left Lori tied up in a cave?" Janet asked loudly. "What if a bear had come back?"

"Relax," Darrin said, taking her pack and pushing her forward. "We've been using this cave for months and have never even seen a chipmunk inside. None of our gear has ever been touched either. It's deserted."

Reaching the entrance, Janet squatted down to peer inside, then duck-walked into the dark cavern. Once inside, she straightened and stood still, waiting for her eyes to adjust. When she could see more, she made out a form lying on the ground to one side of the roomy cavern.

"Lori?" she called. "Is that you?"

The form wriggled and Janet heard a muffled sound. They

must have gagged the girl as well as tied her. Janet hurried forward and, dropping the flowers, knelt beside Lori.

"I'm Deputy Janet Millson," she said quietly as she pulled the gag from Lori's mouth. "I'd like to say I'm here to rescue you, but Bart and Darrin grabbed me too." She untied the young woman's hands and feet as she spoke. "But don't worry, the rest of the sheriff's search party won't be far behind me."

Darrin and Bart followed Janet in. Darrin tossed her pack aside and then the pair of them got busy building a fire on the other side of the cavern.

Lori sat up, rubbing her wrists and ankles. "I'm just glad to see a friendly face," she whispered, "though I'm sorry you're in this situation with me."

Janet smiled. The longer she was in here, the easier it was to see. Lori didn't look like she'd been injured, and except for having been tied and left on her own, seemed to be in good spirits.

Lori's face sobered and she grabbed Janet's arm. "Charlie!" she whispered urgently. "Bart shot Charlie. I'm sure of it. Is… is my brother dead?"

"No," Janet said, quietly but emphatically. "He was airlifted out. He and your father and Luke are all back in Garnet Gateway. Charlie is hospitalized, but he's going to be fine."

Lori sighed with relief and let go of Janet's arm. "Good. That's good."

To take the young woman's mind off her brother's injury, Janet nodded to the men on the other side of the spacious den. "Why are they building the fire over there instead of in the center of the cave?"

"There's a crack in the ceiling over there that acts as a natural chimney," Lori answered, then shrugged. "At least, that's what Darrin said when I asked why the firepit was over there. Seemed like an odd place to put it."

Janet nodded. "They're smarter than I expected. Too bad."

Lori giggled quietly. "At least Darrin is. I'm not too sure about Bart." She scrunched her shoulders and drew up her knees as if to make herself smaller. "Bart is a total creep, but he does whatever Darrin tells him to. Including leaving me alone. At least so far."

Janet put a hand on Lori's shoulder. "Neither of them has... molested you?"

Lori shook her head.

"Good," Janet said. "I'll try everything I know to prevent them from raping either of us, but... you need to be brave, Lori." She paused, and then added, "And be willing to follow my lead if an opportunity presents itself."

A small sob escaped Lori, but she nodded. "I can do that." She sighed and said, "I'm sure glad to know the sheriff is on our trail. I hope he gets here soon."

"You and me both," Janet agreed grimly. "You and me both."

KRISTI LUNDRIGAN REYNOLDS

After their visit to the Richardsons in the hospital, Kristi offered to drive Andrea back to *Delectable Mountain Quilting* so the young woman could retrieve her car and go home.

"Aren't you going back to the shop?" Andrea asked.

"No. I'm going to the sheriff's department to have another chat with Clara."

Andrea slid a look at Kristi from the side of her eye. "Would you mind if I came with you?"

Kristi flicked a startled glance in her direction before returning her attention to the traffic on the street. "Are you sure you want to?" she asked. "It's probably a waste of time since Clara would probably call me if she had news."

"I'd like to come," Andrea said quietly. "I'm invested in this now. Lori is a friend, and Charlie…" Her voice cracked and she stopped, taking a deep breath and holding it for a moment before letting it out in an audible sigh.

Kristi nodded. "I understand. If Jason had been wounded, I'd want answers too." She paused and then asked gently, "Does Charlie know how you feel?"

Andrea sighed again and shook her head. "Not really. I mean, we've been friends forever and he was still in Billings when I first got there. We went out a few times. Not dates exactly. He just included me when a group of his friends were going out somewhere." She fell silent, staring out the passenger window. "I don't know how he feels about me, but I love him." She turned to Kristi, tears sparkling in her eyes. "I can't bear for him to be hurt or in danger."

"Love isn't always easy," Kristi said quietly. "Of course you can come with me to see Clara. We'll do this together."

When they arrived at the department, Clara was on the phone. She waved them into the work area and pointed to a good-sized table. Kristi and Andrea had barely settled in their chairs before the dispatcher joined them.

"What can I do for you ladies?" Clara asked, settling into a chair across from them, a telephone and notepad at her elbow.

"We were wondering if you'd heard anything from Jason," Kristi said.

Clara grimaced. "I was afraid of that."

Kristi's heart raced and she felt sure her expression was startled. "What? What's happened?"

"Well, there's good news, kinda, and there's bad news. Which do you want first?"

Kristi swallowed past the huge lump in her throat, then straightened her shoulders and said, "Give me the bad news. Is Jason hurt?"

Clara stretched her arm across the table and squeezed Kristi's hand. "Nothing like that. Jason is fine. But there has been another shooting. One of the rangers, Hank Lloyd, was injured."

Kristi breathed a sigh of relief, though of course she remained concerned about the ranger's condition. "How bad? Will he be airlifted out?"

Clara shook her head. "No. After Charlie was shot, emergency services left a paramedic with the search team. Good thing, as it turns out. Steve, the paramedic, patched up Hank's shoulder and said he'd be fine to continue with the hunting party." She paused, took a deep breath, and said, "But that's not the really bad news."

Kristi and Andrea both jumped a little in their chairs. "There's more?" asked Andrea.

"The perps captured Janet," Clara said, her expression grim. "They ambushed Janet and Hank, shot Hank, and made off with Janet."

"Oh. My. God," Kristi exclaimed. She couldn't even imagine such a thing. Janet—Jason's most capable deputy—captured and in the hands of the same men who'd taken Lori? Unbelievable. "Jason must be out of his mind!"

"He's pretty riled up," Clara agreed.

Andrea took and deep breath, let it out slowly, and said, "You mentioned good news?"

"Right. The good news. Jason is pretty sure they're holed up in a cave just above the tree line. It's on a rocky slope and there are lots of big boulders to give our guys cover."

Kristi nodded. "And if I know Janet, those creeps will be very sorry to have her behind their lines once she knows Jason and the others are on the scene."

Clara pointed at her. "Exactly!"

Andrea smiled grimly. "Can I ask you something?"

"Of course."

"When I was at the hospital, Luke mentioned that his dad had asked the ranch hands to dig the bullet out of Lori's horse and get it to the sheriff's office. Did they do that?"

Clara nodded. "Yes, one of them brought it in just before lunch. I packaged it up and sent it off to the crime lab. Even better?"

Kristi and Andrea both leaned forward.

"The doctor in Billings who pulled the bullet out of Charlie turned it over to the emergency services guys who brought your brother in. They rushed it straight to the crime lab."

"So the lab has bullets from two incidents to compare," Kristi said quietly, "and one of those, the one involving Charlie, Jason knows for sure where the bullet came from."

"That news will please the sheriff when he gets back," Clara agreed solemnly. "Evidence that ties the same shooter to Lori's abduction and Charlie's injury will help make sure those men spend a lot of time in prison."

"And now they'll have a third bullet," Kristi pointed out. "The one from the ranger."

All three women sat quietly for a few moments considering the implications of the recovery of those bullets.

The phone rang and Clara answered, juggling the receiver and her notepad and pen.

Kristi turned to Andrea, speaking quietly so as not to disturb Clara's concentration. "I was planning to head home after this, but what would you think about going back to the hospital?"

Andrea looked puzzled, but said, "Fine by me. What are we up to?"

Kristi smiled. "I thought you could stay with Charlie while I take Ethan and Luke out to dinner. They need a break, but they won't want to go unless someone stays with Charlie. You game?"

"Absolutely!"

Turning back as Clara finished her call and returned the receiver to its cradle, Kristi said, "I wish we could do something to help the search, but since we can't you can let Jason know we're keeping the Richardsons in the loop."

Clara nodded. "I'll do that the next time he calls in."

They all stood and walked toward the front door.

Kristi paused at the high counter dividing the room into public and work areas and turned to Clara. "You've been here all day. Do you need me to find someone to spell you?"

Clara waved the thought away. "Not necessary. Anita Spencer is my back-up." She glanced at the big round clock that hung on the wall above the front door. "She'll be here in thirty minutes. But thanks for the offer."

"Great," Kristi said. "If you hear anything…"

"You'll be the first call I make," Clara agreed. "Now, go have a nice dinner with Ethan and his boy."

Kristi smiled. "I intend to."

SHERIFF REYNOLDS

Once the other two search teams arrived, Jason and Eli hunkered down to discuss their next move while Steve assessed Hank's condition. The ranger appeared to be doing well. The antibiotics would protect him from the effects of dirt and foreign objects that Steve might have missed when cleaning the wound, and the sling and swathe system had the arm immobilized to protect the shoulder. Finally, the pain meds seemed to be doing their job; Hank was able to stand and walk around the small clearing without assistance.

Eli studied Hank's movement, then turned to Steve. "What's the verdict?"

"I'll keep a close eye on him, but I think he'll be fine to continue with us."

Jason nodded. "Let us know if we're moving too fast, or if he needs more frequent rest stops."

"Hey," Hank growled. "I'm right here. Stop talking about me as if I'm unconscious."

Steve grinned. "See? He's doing fine, but I'll let you know if that changes."

"I'll keep up," Hank said. "It won't be me that keeps us from freeing Janet… and Lori."

"Good enough," Jason said. Raising his voice he addressed the whole team. "If everyone has refilled their canteens, let's move out."

The trail was easy to follow, and a few minutes later the team stopped at the edge of a rocky slope scattered with large boulders and wildflowers.

"Tracking across all that rock could be tricky," Eli said, scanning the hillside while Hank leaned against one of the last ponderosa pines and caught his breath.

"It would be," Adam agreed, "if Janet hadn't left us a few markers."

"What?" Jason asked. "Where?"

"Janet picked flowers as she passed through here," Adam said with a grin. "Look. You can see where stems have been snapped off."

"Maybe you can," Jason said, feeling a little jealous of his deputy's skill. "Okay, Adam, take the lead. Steve and Hank, bring up the rear. Everyone, move quickly and stay as low as possible. Darrin and Bart could be watching from behind any of those boulders. We don't need any more folks with gunshot wounds."

Eli continued to scan the hillside. "I'd guess they're more likely holed up in one of those caves."

"I agree," Hank said. "Looks like Janet's flower trail is heading toward that one." He pointed to what might have been a cave entrance about halfway up the slope. It was small and dark and protected by some large boulders.

"Could be," Adam agreed. "We'll follow the flower trail, but I'll lead us in a zig-zag pattern and we'll move from boulder to boulder to minimize our exposure."

"Good plan," Jason said, nodding and scanning the hillside. Now that Adam had pointed it out, he could see the flower trail, at least the start of it.

Adam and Jason were part way up the hillside when the first shot rang out causing splinters of rock to fly off the boulder the lawmen hid behind. Adam smiled grimly. "Guess that answers the question of whether or not we're heading the right direction."

"Yep," agreed Jason. "Now we also know they're watching the trail. Pick your next boulder carefully."

The rest of the search team was spread out along the hillside below then. They followed Adam and Jason in pairs. Whenever Adam led Jason to another boulder, the next pair moved to the one he and Jason had just left. So far, the tactic was working.

Jason's walkie talkie squawked. He pulled it off his belt and said, "I'm here."

"Did you see where the shot came from?" Eli asked, his voice tinny over the radio.

"No. Did you?"

"As it happens, I did. I saw the muzzle flash. The shooter is hiding behind the boulder just to the left of that low cave we've been angling toward."

Jason nodded and Adam grinned. "Good to know we picked out the right cave."

"Even better that your deputy was smart enough to leave us a trail," Eli said. "She kept us going in the right direction from the start."

"She's the best," Jason agreed. "Let's keep moving. We need to get her back safely. Lori too, of course. Reynolds out."

Adam continued to lead them toward the cave. The team moved low and fast from boulder to boulder. A couple more shots rang out, but no one was hit. When they reached a grouping of several boulders just below the cave, the team was finally able to bunch up with everyone close enough to talk easily.

"Well, we know where they are, but we're pinned down," Eric said. "What's our next move?"

Jason glanced at each team member in turn. "Suggestions?"

CHIEF DEPUTY JANET MILLSON

J anet sat on the cold stone floor of the cave beside Lori. Now that she had the advantage of the flickering light of the fire, she could see that the cave was good-sized, with outcroppings of rock that divided it into several chambers. Not exactly private, but separated enough to provide the illusion of small rooms. One was more closed off than the others.

"What's back there?" she asked Lori, pointing to that section.

Lori made a disgusted face. "That's the toilet area. Darrin showed it to me when we first got here." She paused and lowered her eyes. "I haven't used it," she murmured. "I couldn't bear the idea of taking my pants down when they're around. Bart already looks at me like... well, you know."

Janet touched Lori's arm in sympathy. "We'll go together. I'll stand guard while you use the *facilities*, and you can do the same for me."

Lori nodded. "Thanks."

Janet turned her attention back to studying the cave. She was amazed that their abductors allowed them to sit quietly and talk, but the men seemed preoccupied with tending the fire, keeping watch on the rocky hillside, and bringing in additional firewood.

They were expecting a siege.

Continuing to survey the cave, she noted one section contained several large, plastic storage bins with dented metal buckets nearby. If those contained water, then Jason and his team might have a hard time forcing the men out. Food was another matter, but a body could go without food far longer than it could go without water.

Turning to Lori, Janet said quietly, "We may have to fight to get out of this cave."

Lori looked at her, her blue eyes wide with fear. "Fight?"

Janet nodded.

"But they're such big men! Can't we just wait for rescue? You said the sheriff and his men were close."

"They are," Janet agreed, "but Darrin seems to have this cave set up for a siege. If those big bins are water, they can hold out for a long time. Plus, they have the advantage of being able to watch and shoot down the mountainside... and they have the cover of not only the cave itself, but the boulders outside the entrance. It's a strong position."

Lori nodded. "One we can weaken by distracting them. Maybe even hurting them."

Janet smiled grimly. "Exactly. We'll need to choose our moment. We won't do anything until we know the sheriff and his men are right outside, but we have to be ready. Have you had any training?"

"Kind of," Lori said with a shrug. "I grew up with two older brothers and we fought like cats and dogs when we were younger." She bit her lip before continuing, "Of course, they always knew Dad would tan them if they actually hurt me, so I'm not sure that counts."

Janet tilted her hand back and forth in a so-so gesture. "Anything else?"

"I took a self-defense course in college last year," Lori

answered, "but that's kind of passive. I mean, those techniques are used if someone is attacking me, not the other way around."

"True," Janet agreed, "but you can still use them against one of these two if we get the chance." Janet scooted forward until she could look Lori straight in the eye. "Now, we obviously can't practice, but we can talk our way through an imaginary fight. As long as they leave us alone… and we talk quietly. Tell me some of the techniques you've practiced in class and are fairly comfortable executing."

The two women continued to talk quietly, planning how best to use the self-defense tactics Lori had practiced in her class. They decided that their best chance would be to take on Darrin, two against one. He was taller than Bart, but not as muscular, and if they could get him alone, Janet thought they might have a chance.

But they wouldn't do anything until she knew Jason was right outside and he and his men were keeping Bart pinned down and hiding behind one of the boulders just outside the cave entrance. If she and Lori could take Darrin down, they might have time to crawl through the low opening to the cave and make it past Bart to safety.

Maybe.

Of course, they might also get killed.

God! She hoped she wasn't leading Lori into a fatal exercise. She'd come to rescue the young woman, not put her in danger!

ETHAN RICHARDSON

E than was striding down the hall outside Charlie's hospital room when he spotted Kristi and Andrea approaching.

"Well, hello again," he said when he was close enough to them not to disturb other patients. "Didn't expect to see you two again today."

"Honestly, we didn't expect to visit again today," Kristi said with a smile. "Where are you headed?"

"I'm off to the hospital cafeteria to grab some dinner while Luke sits with Charlie. We'll trade off when I get back."

"Then we're just in time," Kristi said, taking Ethan's arm and turning him back toward Charlie's room. "We stopped and got Andrea something to eat."

Andrea held up the bag holding her submarine sandwich. "I'm going to sit with Charlie while you and Luke go get some dinner with Kristi," she said happily.

"I don't know," Ethan began.

"Ethan, you have to eat. Luke does too," Kristi said sternly. "Andrea will call if anything happens. Besides, it'll do you both good to get out of the hospital for a while."

They'd reached Charlie's room. Ethan beckoned Luke to join them in the hall.

"What's up?" Luke asked, frowning as he glanced from one face to another. "I know you didn't eat this fast."

"Nope," Ethan agreed. "Didn't even make it to the cafeteria." He paused, rubbed the back of his neck and continued. "Kristi and Andrea have this plan for Andrea to sit with Charlie while you and I go out to dinner with Kristi. What do you think?"

Luke glanced at Kristi, and she said the magic word, "Rizzoli's!"

Luke's eyes lit with excitement and he turned to his dad. "Can we? Rizzoli's, Dad!"

Ethan scowled at Kristi. "That was low. Rizzoli's is our favorite restaurant and we haven't eaten there in an age." Hands on hips, he stared at the floor for several seconds before studying Andrea. "You'll call if there's a problem?"

She switched hands with her bag of food and put her right hand over her heart. "I promise. But nothing's going to happen, so you should enjoy your dinner."

Ethan sighed and nodded. Turning to Kristi, he said, "All right. Let's do this."

Luke pumped his fist in the air and let out a muffled whoop. Ethan scowled at him, but didn't scold him for causing a ruckus in the hospital hallway. After all, for Luke, it had been a very quiet whoop.

Kristi winked at Andrea, then turned and gestured down the hall. "This way, gentlemen. My car is right outside."

A short time later Ethan found himself seated at a table in *Rizzoli's Fine Italian Restaurant* with his eldest son and the sheriff's wife. He shook his head. It had been a decidedly strange day. But at least Rizzoli's was as he expected. Its red-checked tablecloths and raffia covered wine bottle candle holders were just as he remembered and he found the soft recorded music soothing to his jangled nerves.

Luke's shoulders had relaxed the moment they stepped over the threshold. Kristi had been right. His son needed this break from the sterile look and smell of the hospital. Truth be told, he did too. Ethan took a deep breath—inhaling the enticing aromas of rich tomato sauce replete with garlic and oregano and sizzling meats—and felt his own shoulders relax.

All three were studying the menu when Mama Rizzoli bustled to their table. She rested a hand on Ethan's shoulder and said, "We heard about your troubles, Ethan. Your money is no good here tonight."

Ethan shook his head. "I can't let you do that, Louisa. This restaurant is your livelihood."

"Our restaurant is doing just fine, Ethan Richardson," she said with a smile. "Salvatore and I already agreed that we would provide food for your family while you're dealing with this crisis." She turned to Kristi. "You have a food train set up?"

"We do. I'll give you Andrea's number. She's in charge."

"Andrea Jansson?" Mama asked, then nodded. "She's a good girl." Turning to Luke, she asked, "What can I get you, young man?"

"I'll have the spaghetti and meatballs," he said quickly.

When Mama had taken their order, she bustled back to the kitchen and a server approached with a basket of focaccia bread, a bowl of warm olive oil, and glasses of ice cold water.

"Enjoy," she said. "Mama will bring your dinners out shortly."

Ethan broke off a piece of bread, dipped it in the oil, and savored the first bite. He swallowed, dabbed his lips with his napkin, and said, "I'm truly humbled by all the care everyone is providing to us." He ticked off his points on his fingers. "Our room at the Inn is practically free, Andrea is sitting with Charlie and eating a sandwich while we're here enjoying this meal, people from all over the community have signed up to provide food for us, and your husband and his deputies are out in the wilderness searching for our girl." He shook his head. "And don't tell me it's their job. It's still greatly appreciated."

Luke nodded his agreement, his eyes somber.

Kristi reached across the table and patted Ethan's hand. "Garnet Gateway is a caring community and your family is an integral part. Everyone is concerned for Lori and Charlie and they want to help. Let them."

Ethan nodded and took another bite of bread.

"Besides," Kristi continued, "I know your family will pay it forward to whoever the next folks are to find themselves in trouble. As for Jason and his deputies, they're the best at what they do. They'll find Lori and bring her home and will consider it a privilege to have done so."

At that moment, Mama returned carrying a folding stand and followed by a young man carrying a tray loaded with steaming dishes which he placed on the stand Mama set up.

"Shrimp Alfredo for our Kristi," Mama said as she place a serving of glorious fettuccine noodles smothered in creamy, cheesy white sauce with perfectly sautéed shrimp in front of Kristi.

Kristi's eyes widened and she licked her lips. "Thank you, Mama!"

"And for our young Luke, plenty of spaghetti and meatballs." She winked at him. "Young men need lots of energy."

Luke stared at the huge plate of spaghetti loaded with rich tomato sauce and giant meatballs. He barely glanced at Mama as he murmured, "Thanks," and grabbed his fork.

"And finally, for our dear friend Ethan. Salvatore and I hope that this lasagna not only fills your stomach, but also soothes your worries and comforts you." She placed his plate before him, and said, "Lasagna is my go-to comfort food. May it be the same for you."

"I don't know how it couldn't be," Ethan said. "It looks and smells absolutely wonderful, Louisa. Please thank Salvatore for me as well."

Mama patted his shoulder. "I will, and when your family is whole and healthy once more come back to see us."

Tears pricked Ethan's eyes, but he didn't allow them to fall. "Thank you, Louisa. We'll do that."

Kristi had been right to bring them to Rizzoli's. He and Luke needed the food, but they needed the comfort of community even more.

24

SHERIFF REYNOLDS

Sheriff Jason Reynolds and his search team settled in to wait the perps out though it was only late afternoon. Jason assigned a watch rotation to make sure neither Darrin nor Bart left the cave, and to assure their own safety.

"Well," he said, "since we're not going anywhere at the moment, we might as well get comfortable." His men glanced at him quizzically, then shrugged and pulled lightweight blankets and sleeping pads from their packs.

Jason rubbed his face, then brightened. "Hey, we still have some of those sandwiches Kristi sent, don't we? Let's divvy them up and call it dinner."

Since only Jason and his original two deputies had eaten sandwiches earlier and Kristi had sent an even dozen, they *almost* had enough for everyone. The missing sandwich was in Janet's pack, and the nine men hoped she and Lori would be able to enjoy it.

Steve and Hank split one sandwich and one of the apples, but declined the cookie. Eric ate his sandwich and apple while on watch, but kept his cookie for later. Everyone else ate everything they were given and silently thanked Kristi for her thoughtfulness.

Jason went over the watch rotation again after cautioning the men to remember who came after them. "Let's get some rest while we can. Wake your replacement when it's time to change the watch, but otherwise, get as much sleep as you can. When it gets dark, we'll discuss our options. I want them focused on us overnight, not the women."

The men grumbled, but stretched out as best they could without leaving the cover of the boulders. Eli brought his belongings over to rest beside Jason.

"What do you have in mind for the night?" he asked.

"Not sure yet," Jason replied quietly, "but the men's brains will be working the problem while they sleep. Maybe one of them will come up with a brilliant idea."

Eli grunted, then said doubtfully, "I suppose..."

Jason gave the ranger a grim smile. "I can hope. Now, get some sleep. Who knows, maybe that great idea will be yours."

Eli chuckled and shook his head. "You're a dreamer, Jason, but I like that about you."

Jason slid down on his pad, pulled his Stetson over his eyes, and said, "I sure can be." After all, he thought as his eyes closed, I wouldn't have won Kristi back if I hadn't dreamed I could!

It felt like he'd barely gotten comfortable when Roger shook him awake. "Sorry boss," his deputy said quietly, "but it's your watch."

Jason sat up, rubbed his face, and settled his Stetson firmly on his head. "Thanks, Roger. Get some rest." He took up the guard position, a spot between the boulders that was well protected but provided an unobstructed view of the cave entrance.

He glanced at the sky. It was beautiful, clear night. The sun had just set, painting the western sky with vibrant colors—oranges, pinks, and purples, even a streak of pure red. Fortunately, the twilight sky still provided enough light to see the cave easily, but that wouldn't last much longer.

It was almost time to get everyone up to discuss their options.

As he watched, one of the perps scurried out of the cave on all fours. The man ran to one of the nearby boulders and disappeared. A moment later another man, this one stockier and heavier, left the protection of the boulder and scurried inside.

Jason nodded to himself. Now he knew which boulder they were using as a sniper nest.

Good to know. He could use that information.

Time to wake his team and plan their next move.

25

CHIEF DEPUTY JANET MILLSON

Lori's stomach growled loudly, and Janet realized she was hungry as well. As nonchalantly as possible, she stood and walked toward the section of the cave where she'd seen Darrin toss her pack earlier. Though she moved quietly, both men turned to look at her.

"Where do you think you're going?" Darrin asked.

"I want my pack," she said, standing still and placing her fists on her hips. "Lori and I are hungry and I have a canteen and some energy bars in my pack." She paused before continuing in a sneering voice, "Unless you plan to fix us dinner, that is."

Bart went back to cleaning his rifle, but Darrin continued staring at her. He nudged Bart. "You searched her pack, right?"

Bart glanced up. "Yep. Nothing in there that could count as a weapon."

Darrin nodded and waved her on. "Fine. Get your pack. Bart and I don't need your energy bars."

Glaring at him, Janet retrieved her pack and strode back to where Lori huddled against the cave wall.

"Do you really have food?" she asked, shivering slightly.

"Yes," Janet answered, rummaging around in the roomy pack

she pulled out a lightweight blanket. "And I have this." She draped the soft material around Lori's shoulders. "You look cold. They shouldn't have left you on cold stone when they tied you up. Pretty sure I saw camp pads over there. One of those would've offered some protection from the chill."

"Thanks," Lori said. "I am a bit cold."

Janet nodded and pulled out the sandwich Kristi had given her before she left Garnet Gateway. Unwrapping it, she noted that it was already cut in half. That solved one problem. She pulled the apple and cookie from the pack and placed them beside the sandwich.

"There," she said. "A veritable feast!"

Lori giggled.

"I'd slice the apple in half, but," she shrugged, "no knife and I'm not asking for one."

"Good," Lori agreed. "They might take the food." She nodded to the meal. "That's not an energy bar."

"Too true," Janet said, breaking the cookie in half before grabbing her canteen and adding it to the food between them. "We'll just have to share the apple and the canteen."

"Works for me," Lori said cheerfully. "Sharing germs with you doesn't concern me. Now Bart..." She didn't finish the thought, but picked up her half of the sandwich and took a big bite. "Mmmm," she murmured, closing her eyes and leaning her head back against the stone wall. "Smoked ham and provolone. Nice."

Janet bit into her half, chewed, and swallowed. After taking a swig of water, she said, "Could use a bit of mayonnaise, but these were made for hiking. If you carry them too long, mayo isn't safe."

"I'm not complaining," Lori said after drinking from the canteen. "You wouldn't believe what I fixed for lunch at that first campsite."

"I saw the skillet and the firepit," Janet said. "Too bad you didn't manage to brain one of them. Cast iron makes a formidable weapon."

"I thought about it," Lori said, "but then I heard Charlie yell and Bart shot that rifle and Darrin grabbed me." She shivered again, but Janet doubted it was from cold this time. "I was so panicked about Charlie that I forgot about attacking. I just wanted to get to my brother."

Janet patted her arm. "Don't worry about it. Charlie is safe and you've done a great job of staying alive." She popped the last bite of sandwich in her mouth. "That's the most important thing you could've done. We want to rescue you, not retrieve your corpse."

Lori nodded, then eyed the apple.

"Go ahead," Janet said with an encouraging smile. "I've eaten more regularly today than you have."

"If you want a bite, just say so." Lori grabbed the apple and bit in. A little juice dribbled down her chin and she grabbed the napkin the sandwich had been wrapped in and wiped it away.

Janet picked up her half of the cookie and nibbled an edge. Oatmeal raisin. One of her favorites. Plus, the tasty treat was packed with energy, which Janet was sure they'd need before the night was over.

She studied the men across the cave as they cleaned their weapons and checked their ammunition. She saw three deer rifles and at least two handguns, one of them hers. If she could just get her hands on one of those guns....

She sighed. She'd just have to hope that once Jason and the others showed up she'd find an opportunity. Or maybe she'd make one.

For now, she encouraged Lori to rest.

26

KRISTI LUNDRIGAN REYNOLDS

Kristi was exhausted by the time she stepped through her back door into her kitchen. Not just physically, but mentally and emotionally. It had been a long day filled with other people's heartache and her own worry.

She chided herself as her moggy cats, Stitches and Between trotted into the kitchen to greet her. Truly, not so much worry as concern. Jason could handle himself; he'd proved that during several murder investigations over the last couple of years. Murder investigations that she'd been only too involved in.

But Jason had solved those horrible crimes and Garnet Gateway had reverted to its normal laid-back existence. The worst Jason and his deputies had needed to deal with recently was bored teens and lost dogs. Kristi preferred that type of crime. The kind where her husband wasn't in any danger.

"All right, kitty-kids," she said, reaching down to stroke each of the cats in turn. "Let's get you some dinner while you distract me from my concern over my more-than-capable husband."

Stitches and Between practically danced over to the low cupboard where the cat food and their dishes were stored. Kristi poured kibble into their bowls and placed them on the floor before opening the refrigerator and fixing herself a glass of iced tea.

Leaning against the counter, she sipped her tea and watched her cats. They'd been great company during her estrangement from Jason. She'd adopted Stitches first, the gray tabby female with four white paws had stolen her heart at first sight. Later, she'd made the mistake of visiting the shelter, just to drop off a donation of cat food and litter, and had seen Between. The tiny tuxedo male with the personality of a perennial kitten had met her gaze, meowed to her, and melted her heart. She'd been an instant goner.

Being a quilter, Kristi had named her new companions for her craft. Stitches was an obvious choice, but Between often confused people. He was so named because his sharp little claws reminded her of the tiny, sharp needles used in hand quilting.

Whatever. She wasn't concerned about what other people thought of her cats' names, only that she and her kitty-kids were happy with them!

Carrying her glass of iced tea with her, she wandered through the dining room and into the living room. The house felt oddly empty. Funny that. Prior to the wedding last Thanksgiving, she and the cats had been the only occupants of this cozy house, and they were all present now. But Jason was missing, and he took up an enormous place in her heart and home.

That wasn't strange at all. Jason was the love of her life! Even after she'd divorced him for infidelity, she'd still loved him. She'd mourned their broken relationship, but she'd never deluded herself about his place in her heart.

She'd purchased this house after their divorce. She'd wanted a new start, and, much like her adoption of the cats, Kristi had recognized this house as hers the moment she stepped over the threshold. Everything about it suited her, from its views of the Absaroka Range from the breakfast nook window to the number of bedrooms. Three. Allowing her a master bedroom, a guest bedroom, and her all-important quilting studio.

She loved this house and hadn't wanted to part with it. Jason had agreed, and so, rather than hunting for a place the two of them could buy together, she'd made room for him in her home. It hadn't been hard. Jason wasn't really into decorating. His furniture was minimal and his kitchen equipment laughable. With a few tweaks, her home had become *their* home... and now it felt empty without him.

Settling on the couch, she thought about turning on the television for company, but Stitches and Between jumped lightly up beside her demanding attention.

"Who needs TV?" she asked them with a laugh. "I'd much rather visit with the two of you."

Stitches kneaded Kristi's leg gently—the little tabby was always careful of her claws around Kristi—while Between batted at a lock of her shoulder-length blonde hair. Kristi stroked them each in turn until Stitches curled up beside her and closed her eyes and Between sprawled on her lap belly-up so she could rub his softest fur.

"You two are the best kitty-kids a woman could have." Feeling content at last, Kristi reached for the remote control, switched on the big-screen television Jason had brought with him, and found a Victorian romance movie to while away the hours until bedtime.

Glancing at Jason's tan leather recliner, she hoped he was safe and had found a reasonably comfortable place to sleep tonight. She *really* hoped he'd find the Richardson girl and be home tomorrow.

With a sigh, she turned her attention to the movie and immersed herself in appreciation of the elaborate sets and costumes. No matter the time period, life went on.

27

SHERIFF REYNOLDS

Sheriff Jason Reynolds didn't like the fact that night was quickly approaching. Visibility would be lost and possibly worse, the perps would be thinking of bedding down. He couldn't afford to let them get comfortable. Not if he wanted to get Janet and Lori back unharmed. He knew without a doubt as the darkness descended, Bart and Darrin would be thinking of using the women to calm their sexual appetites.

"Okay, men," he said, quietly gathering his team's attention. "We need to figure out how to keep the perps engaged overnight. We can't give them the time and space to think about Janet and Lori as sex objects. Ideas?"

The men growled to themselves, but it was Evan who spoke up. "I'd suggest taking pot shots at the sniper's rock at odd intervals," he said before shaking his head, "but we can't afford to waste ammunition."

"True," Liam said. "But what about rocks? Any of you guys have a decent throwing arm? I was a pitcher for my high school baseball team, and I've kept up with the skill."

Hank nodded. "There are plenty of rocks on the ground around us, and once it's full dark we can move out carefully and scout for more." He glanced mournfully at the sling wrapping his arm to his chest. "I'm out for throwing, but I can search for additional ammo."

Steve patted Hank's good shoulder. "You gather, I'll throw for the both of us." He turned to Jason. "I can hit a target with a baseball. I'm sure I can hit that boulder with a rock."

Jason nodded. "We wouldn't even have to hit the boulder or the cave entrance. Just lobbing a rock out that makes a noise against the rocky ground will make them wonder what we're up to, and that's what we want. We want them awake and nervous."

"Sounds like a plan," Eli said. "Let's continue with two men on guard duty. They can take turns watching for movement and tossing rocks to worry them."

"Good enough," Jason agreed. "Adam, you'll join me on the first watch, though I have a scouting mission in mind for you. Liam and Eric, you'll follow us. Roger and Eli, you'll be up after them. Evan and Steve, you're in reserve. Hank, I want you resting. Steve, get as much rest as you can. No telling what tomorrow will bring and you're our only medic."

Steve glanced at Hank and the two of them nodded to each other.

Jason signaled to Adam, and in the fading light, they separated themselves from their fellows. Adam raised his eyebrows in a silent question.

"About that scouting mission," Jason began, "as soon as full dark falls, I want you to move uphill and see what you can find. Is there another way into that cave? It looked like they had a fire earlier. Is there a chimney we can plug and smoke them out?"

Adam rubbed his forehead, but nodded. "It'd be easier to make out in the daylight—especially the smoke, but I'll see what I can find."

"Good man," Jason said and clasped his shoulder for a moment.

After Adam moved away to set up his bedroll, Jason took a moment to study the men who were on this hunt with him.

Adam Brooks was new to Jason's team, having last worked in Missoula. The man was older than most of Jason's deputies, but he'd proven both skillful and dependable on this manhunt. He was an asset to Jason's department and the sheriff was glad he'd had the good sense to hire the man.

Eric Lawson. Jason smiled as he watched the young man check in with the other team members. Now there was a dependable deputy. Eric had been with the department since Jason had first been elected to his office. Eric and Janet were the backbone of the department. Whatever needed to be done, they were right there, digging in.

Evan Knott and Roger Jepperson had joined the department together. They'd been friends since grade school and had grown up on neighboring ranches just outside Garnet Gateway. The two had gone off to college together, studied criminal justice, and after graduation had joined the Billings police department. But they were Garnet Gateway men, so when Jason was granted permission to expand his team, they both applied. Jason hired them at their first interview. They knew the inhabitants of the valley and had a stake in the county's well-being.

Yes. These men—plus Janet, of course—constituted a department any sheriff could be proud of. Jason had helped build a capable and trustworthy department.

He turned his attention to the men he hadn't known before this manhunt started: the paramedic and the law enforcement rangers.

He'd lucked out there. Beartooth Ranger District had sent him three excellent men. While he hadn't known them long, Jason felt he could trust Eli, Liam, and Hank with his life. More importantly he could trust them with Lori and Janet's lives.

Lt. Steve Jeffers had already proved himself invaluable. Jason was very much afraid that if the paramedic hadn't been along

Hank would have died of his wound. Shaking his head, Jason sincerely hoped Steve's skills wouldn't be needed again before the kidnappers were in custody and the women were safe.

He rested his head against a boulder and closed his eyes for a moment. Whatever came next, he had the best team available. They would prevail. No matter what.

28

DEPUTY ADAM BROOKS

I t was full dark when Adam slid from behind their sheltering boulders and began his slow ascent of the slope. Despite the darkness, he had a decent view of where he was going and where he placed his feet. He'd always been blessed with good night vision and tonight he'd waited until his eyes adjusted to the dark before setting out.

He recognized the danger of this assignment. There wasn't much cover until he got far enough up the slope to move above the cave entrance. If one of the perps also had good night vision, Adam could be shot. It was a risk, but one he was willing to take.

He respected Sheriff Reynolds. He'd liked the man when he'd interviewed for the job, but now that he'd worked with him in the field that initial liking had turned to respect for a skilled lawman and a born leader. Adam was proud that, though he was the newest member of the sheriff's team, his boss had trusted him enough to ask him to make this scouting run.

Adam had made a good decision to leave Missoula and relocate to Garnet Gateway. Jason Reynolds was a sheriff he could trust. He'd learn a lot from this department. Maybe enough to run his own unit someday.

Not in Garnet County. Not unless Jason Reynolds retired. No way would Adam disrespect the man by campaigning to take his job. But in a few years, when he felt he'd learned enough, maybe he'd try for a sheriff's position in another county.

Moving slowly and silently up the slope, Adam smiled at himself and put his future ambitions away. He could dream about all that later. Right now he needed to concentrate on moving silently and learning all he could about the perps' stronghold.

When he drew level with the cave he was able to make out the niche behind the boulder beside the opening... the spot they were using as a sniper's nest. Crouched low against the rocky hillside, he remained still long enough to watch one of the men duck-walk out of the low entrance and move sideways into position in that niche.

They were vulnerable for a moment when they changed the guard. Good to know.

Adam stayed motionless while the man settled into his position. Once the sniper's attention was firmly on the boulders behind which the rest of Adam's team took refuge, Adam moved on.

Once he was on the slope above the cave, he continued to place his feet with extreme care. A sound cracked from the slope below him and he froze, then he grinned. The sheriff had started lobbing rocks at the cave. That first one had sounded almost like a gunshot in the stillness of the night. Glancing down on the sniper's nest, he saw that the perp was on alert, his rifle at his shoulder, swinging it slowly around as he searched for a target.

Good thing Adam was already above him. Otherwise he might have been spotted. The sheriff's timing was excellent.

Turning his attention back to his assignment, Adam sniffed the air. He detected a slight pungent odor of burning brush. They must have a fire going in the cave. Since he hadn't noticed the smell when he was level with the cave entrance, Adam figured there must be a natural chimney nearby. But where?

Turning his head from side to side, he thought the odor might be stronger to his left. He sidled in that direction and found that it did intensify slightly. Letting his nose guide him, Adam found where the smoke was escaping the cave—a crack in the rock below his feet. Not a big crack, nothing you'd notice just walking around in daylight, but it was about a half-inch wide and about two feet long. Too bad he didn't have any extra fabric with him. Not even a jacket he could sacrifice to stuff the crack and smoke the perps out.

Sighing, he noted the position of the 'chimney' and moved on. He needed to see if he could locate a secondary entrance to the perps' stronghold.

After another forty-five minutes or so of searching, Adam gave up. He'd found nothing other than the crack that acted as a natural chimney. Time to make his way back to camp and report to the sheriff. He wished he had better news, but it was what it was.

Silently, Adam made his way back to the boulders sheltering his team.

29

CHIEF DEPUTY JANET MILLSON

As the sun went down, the cave got darker. If Darrin hadn't kept the fire burning, Janet wouldn't have been able to see Lori. The chief deputy despised feeling grateful to their abductors for anything, but she was glad of the fire. Not only did it provide a little light, it also took the edge off the cold that seeped into the space from the rock walls and floor.

After the women used the semi-private recess that had been designated as a latrine, they shuffled around on the way back to their sitting area and found a couple of rocks that fit their hands well enough to use as weapons should the need arise. Once back in their assigned places, Janet pulled a camp pad from her pack, spread it out on the cold rock floor, and urged Lori to stretch out.

"Don't worry, Lori, I'll stay awake. You can sleep. If I need you, I'll wake you."

"But you can't stay awake all night," Lori exclaimed quietly. "You need rest too."

Janet shook her head. "I've been trained to stay alert. I'll be fine. Besides, if I need sleep, I'll wake you and you can take over guard duty."

"Well, at least sit on the end of the pad. I won't need the whole length."

When Janet agreed and moved onto the insulating surface of the pad, Lori reluctantly curled up to sleep, pulling the light-weight blanket Janet had provided earlier over herself.

Janet noticed that Lori kept her fist-sized rock tucked close against her body. Good. She'd have a weapon if Janet had to wake her into a struggle.

Sitting cross-legged on the end of the mat, Janet watched Darrin. He was the only perp in the cave at the moment. Bart was evidently on watch outside. Janet had noticed a couple of large boulders near the entrance of the cave when she'd arrived, but she hadn't been allowed time to make a good assessment of their potential as hiding places.

She hoped Jason and the rest of the search party were nearby by now. She knew Hank and Adam were excellent trackers, but Hank was injured and she had no idea whether or not he'd survived. She hoped he had. She'd enjoyed working with the ranger and had a lot of respect for him as a fellow lawman.

Regardless of Hank's condition, Jason wouldn't abandon Lori and he certainly wouldn't abandon Janet. The able-bodied men would continue the search, and she'd done everything in her power to leave them a trail. She only wished she had some idea where they were right now.

Much as she hated to admit it, Janet was getting nervous. Night had fallen. The world was quiet outside the cave. She and Lori were vulnerable. Darrin and Bart had kidnapped them because of their sex; it was only a matter of time before the men decided to rape them… and the dead of night in a cold cave seemed like a great time for the men to demand the warmth of female bodies.

Only Janet had no intention of allowing them to use her or Lori in that way. She'd die before she allowed either of them to be raped.

Darrin turned toward them and eyed Janet. She could almost hear him calculating his odds, when a sharp report sounded from beyond the entrance.

Janet sat up straighter. Had that been a gun shot? A footstep dislodging a rock on the slope? What? Something unexpected, that was certain.

Darrin jumped to his feet. He approached the entrance cautiously, and called out, "Bart? You okay? What was that?"

Bart's voice was muffled by distance, and Janet strained to hear his reply.

"Not sure. I don't see anything. They're out there, I saw them moving around before we lost the light. But they're not lighting any fires. No clue what they're doing now."

"Was it a gun shot?"

"I don't think so. Didn't sound quite right. But noise echoes weird with all this rock around us."

Darrin settled near the opening. "Okay. I'll stay close. Yell if you need me to come out."

Janet smiled. Her team was close. She'd be ready when the sheriff made his move.

SHERIFF REYNOLDS

A dam slipped behind the boulder next to Jason and gently tapped the sheriff's shoulder. Jason startled, but didn't turn his weapon on his newest deputy. Instead, he glanced at him sideways.

"You're good," he said. "I've been studying that slope watching for you. Didn't see a thing."

Adam shrugged. "I have excellent night vision which makes placing my feet carefully much easier." He grinned. "But if you didn't see me, when you knew I was out there, it means the perps were unlikely to have seen me either."

"True enough," Jason agreed with a nod. "What did you find out?"

"I found the chimney. It's a natural crack in the rock and small enough to plug with fabric, but I didn't have anything with me. If we want to do that, I'll have to back with supplies."

Jason turned back to studying the slope. "I'll give that some thought. What else?"

"That's it. No other entrances. Though I was just above the entrance when you lobbed that first stone. The sniper straightened up sharpish. I thought he might fire that rifle, but he controlled himself." He paused when Jason handed him a canteen, swallowed some water, and continued, "Got the other guy's attention too. I heard him questioning the sniper from inside the cave. Couldn't make out his words, but the tone was anxious."

"Good to know it drew the inside guy's attention too." Jason glanced at his deputy. "You did well. Now, wake Liam and Eric and then get some sleep yourself. I'll rest as soon as those two take over for me."

"Will do."

A few minutes later Eric and Liam moved into position for the next watch, and Jason sidled out of their way.

"Adam reports that throwing rocks puts the perps on alert," Jason said, "so keep that up. But don't do it too regularly. We don't want them to get comfortable enough to ignore the sound."

"Got it," Eric said. "Don't worry, Sheriff. We've got this."

Jason nodded. "I know you do. Wake me if you need me." With that he moved quietly to the spot where he'd laid out his bedroll. He wasn't really sleepy; it was too early and his mind was crowded with worry. Was Janet okay? How was Lori holding up? What was Kristi doing? What would their best tactic be in the morning? Was Hank really well enough to continue? Should he have figured out how to get the ranger to a hospital? What time in the morning should he take that next step? He didn't want to wait until the sun was up. Perhaps 4:00 a.m. The kidnappers should be worn out by that time, and it would still be dark enough to cover Jason's team's movements. Now all he needed was a plan.

He stretched out, pulled his Stetson over his face, and tried to quiet his mind. Didn't matter what time it was. Didn't matter what the small hours of the morning would bring. If he wasn't rested, he wouldn't be at his best. And Janet and Lori were counting on his best. As were his men.

Taking several deep breaths and releasing them slowly, he

tried to relax. What was the old standby? Oh, yeah. Counting sheep. He smiled. Not likely, but he could count endearing things he'd seen Kristi's cats do.

Stitches stretched across the back of the couch, her head touching Kristi's shoulder.

Between pouncing on his feet when Jason repositioned his legs in bed.

Stitches winding back and forth between his legs when he came home from work.

Between chasing a feather that had escaped from one of the decorative pillows in the living room.

With a quiet snort of amusement, Jason slipped into much needed sleep. Accompanied by two cats he never would have adopted on his own, but they were his by marriage now. And tonight, they'd done him a real service.

Tomorrow's problems would come soon enough. For now, Sheriff Jason Reynolds slept.

BART BLAKESLEY

While Jason slept, Bart fumed.

This wasn't how the night was supposed to go! He had his female. Hell, they'd even managed to grab a woman for Darrin. But were either of them enjoying the delights of soft flesh and hot sex?

No. They were not.

At least he wasn't... and Darrin damn well better not be getting any either. Not when Bart was stuck out here behind a boulder keeping an eye on the lawmen camped out there below their cave.

Damnation! He wanted that little female. He'd been watching her perfectly toned ass all day. She was packed nicely into those blue jeans. He'd enjoyed the sight, but now he wanted to peel off the denim and find out just how firm that little ass was when he put his hands on her.

And was he doing that? Was he tearing the clothes off of her and pushing his rock-hard cock into her pulsing pussy?

No. He. Was. Not!

He was sitting out here with only his thoughts and his rifle for company.

And it was all that sheriff's fault.

If that posse wasn't on their tail, he'd be getting his fill of hers.

A crack sounded on the rock beside his head.

Damn! That was too close.

He pushed thoughts of the female from his mind, raised his rifle, and searched the slope below him for a target.

Nothing.

The posse was wasting ammunition. They couldn't see in the dark any better than he could. Certainly not well enough to actually shoot him. Still, that last shot had been too close.

Bart was tired of being on watch, but he knew he was a decent sniper. If any of the posse tried to sneak up on them, he'd nail them. Darrin wouldn't have a chance of making the shot in the dark. Darrin's night vision sucked and he wasn't that good with a rifle to begin with.

Not like Bart.

Bart had trained with a paramilitary group for a while. He'd done well enough on the shooting range that the commander had singled him out for sniper training. He'd tried for the real military, but the recruiter had dismissed him. The man had put it on Bart's record that his personality was 'suspect.' Whatever the hell that meant.

Still, he'd gotten the training he wanted. And without having to give up years of his life obeying stupid orders. He was a great shot, had no trouble shooting game or people, and could do what needed to be done when it was needed.

Poor Darrin was in there trying to figure out an escape route. The cave was a great place to hole up for the winter, but a lousy spot to retreat from. Especially with armed lawmen camped just down the slope.

Whatever. Darrin would figure it out. He always did.

They'd met at that paramilitary camp. While Bart was learning the ins and outs of killing, Darrin had been training in tactics. The commander had decided he had the makings for rank. Unfortunately, neither Darrin nor Bart had been interested in sticking with the group long term. They'd formed a bond and struck out on their own, stealing and terrorizing people across three states.

Their path wasn't random. Darrin had a plan. He led Bart to the Beartooth Highway, and from there deep into the Absaroka-Beartooth Wilderness. That had been two years ago. They'd spent the time since developing their two camps, one for summer and the cave for winter.

Finally, Darrin had decreed that it was time to find themselves a woman. Someone to cook for them, satisfy their needs, and generally make life worth living.

They'd succeeded, but that damn posse was screwing everything up. They'd expected to melt into the 'Sorkees with no one the wiser about where they went. That hadn't worked out so well, and while the posse had provided a second woman, Darrin hadn't figured out how to deal with the rest of the lawmen yet.

Bart was all for running in while they slept, guns blazing. But Darrin nixed that idea. They didn't know how many lawmen were chasing them or how they kept finding them. Darrin had been careful. That wading through the water should've done the trick, but the posse hadn't lost their trail. At the very least, the posse had some really good trackers.

Even if they managed to get away from the cave with the women—who were bound to slow them down and try to escape—Bart didn't have a clue where they'd go next. They'd only had two camps ready, and now both were known to the law.

Damn it all! This wasn't how things were supposed to happen. He should be pounding Lori into the ground by now, not sitting out here while the posse took pot shots at him.

He growled to himself. Everything was just *wrong*!

Darrin had damn well better come up with a plan. One that would work this time.

3 2

SHERIFF REYNOLDS

The wee small hours of the morning found Jason and Eli discussing tactics. They decided on a course of action and quietly woke the rest of the team.

"All right, men," Jason said quietly when they were all gathered around him. "Grab your canteens and an energy bar for breakfast. You can eat while I lay out the plan Eli and I came up with."

After a bit of turmoil while everyone found their packs and rifled through them for food, the search party once again settled down to listen intently to Jason's words.

"Eli and I think we should attack the cave while it's still dark and from three different directions," Jason said. Pointing a flashlight on low beam at the ground, he used a finger-length piece of stone to draw a rough map in the dirt, having cleared the space earlier to give himself a canvas.

Pointing to a curved symbol, he continued, "This is the cave, and here is the sniper nest." Drawing a set of Xs, he said. "Here's where we are. Now, we're going to break into three teams."

He drew a number one behind the Xs. "Team one will stay

131

here and keep the sniper busy, preferably by throwing rocks, but using bullets if necessary."

Drawing a long, sweeping line from the Xs to the far side of the sniper nest, he wrote a number two beside it. "The second team will circle around to the side and flank the sniper. Once they're in position they'll wait for my signal before engaging." He glanced up and met each man's gaze. "We want to bring them in alive, but don't take any chances. If you have to shoot to kill to save yourself or someone else, do it."

Finally, he drew a line from the Xs to a spot beyond the mark representing the cave. "Team three will make their way up the slope and get above the cave entrance. The first two teams will concentrate on the sniper. The third team will get inside, subdue the second perp, and make sure the women are safe."

He glanced around again. "Any questions?"

The men shook their heads. Roger asked the obvious question, "What are our team assignments?"

Jason nodded. Good men. They weren't arguing or challenging the tactics, just asking who was expected to do what.

"Team one will be Evan, Steve, and Hank. The whole plan hinges on you three. The sniper can keep the other two teams pinned down if you don't manage to get his attention and hold it."

Evan traded glances with Steve and Hank. "Got it, boss. We'll get you the cover you need."

Jason nodded and pointed to the line with the number two on it. "Team two will be Eric, Roger, and Eli. Subduing the sniper is your responsibility. Team one is unlikely to get a clear line of sight on him. We'll be counting on you three to find one and knock him out of his nest."

All three men nodded. "Got it," they said in unison.

"That leaves Adam, Liam, and me to get the drop on the man in the cave with the women." Jason met Adam's gaze. "I saved you for this team since you've already made this trek before. Liam and I will be counting on you to lead us by the quickest path with the best coverage from the sniper. Darkness will help, but I know you'll find the best cover for us."

"Understood, Sheriff."

Eli spoke up. "All right. Everyone knows their assignment. Get your gear packed, but leave everything but your weapons here. Check your ammunition and if you have a knife, bring it, just in case. We aren't expecting hand-to-hand fighting, but then we weren't expecting to lose Janet to these criminals."

Jason nodded his agreement. "We have a plan, and we think it's a good one. But plans go awry. This will be a fluid situation. Get ready, confer with your teammates. We'll implement on my mark."

He looked around, meeting each man's gaze, then nodded. "Stay safe. Secure your targets. And good hunting."

33

CHIEF DEPUTY JANET MILLSON

Janet woke with a start. She'd kept watch for most of the night, but had finally admitted she needed some sleep. She'd awakened Lori a little after midnight and traded off the watch. She'd also warned Lori that the search team was close and they were shooting, or doing something else, to keep the perps focused outside the cave.

Janet rubbed her eyes and studied the cave. Everything was as it had been when she fell asleep, the night was still black beyond the low opening. Lori sat beside her; Darrin hunkered down near the entrance, and the fire still burned, though it looked like it might go out if not tended. It needed to have new fuel added.

"Morning," Janet said, letting Lori know she was awake. "Let's use the latrine while we have the chance. I have the feeling things are going to move quickly as soon as it's morning."

Lori nodded and the two women moved to the somewhat private section of the cave and took care of business. Darrin glanced their direction once, noted where they were headed and turned back to the entrance, effectively ignoring them.

Once the women had returned to the sleeping pad Janet shook her canteen, decided they had enough water to allow energy bars to go down easily. She really didn't want to call enough attention to herself to ask Darrin to refill the canteen. She was sure at least one of the bins she'd noticed held water, but she was loathe to remind the kidnapper of their presence.

Handing Lori the canteen and an energy bar, Janet opened her own and ate. It wasn't bad, though she was really looking forward to having a real meal again soon. The chewy bar reminded her of the granola bars her mom used to give her as an after-school snack. Toasted oats, honey, a few spices. Not bad... but it couldn't compare to the delights of crisp bacon, over-easy eggs, and lightly toasted sourdough bread! She closed her eyes as she chewed, imagining the breakfast she wasn't having.

"What now?" Lori asked quietly, handing the canteen to Janet. "Any ideas?"

Janet swallowed a mouthful of water and capped the canteen before answering. "Now we wait." She met Lori's doubtful gaze with a determined one of her own. "I know that's what we've been doing, but it's different now. We know the search party is out there. We know Darrin and Bart are worried."

"We do?"

Janet nodded. "If they weren't concerned, we'd have been fighting them off all night. No, they're focused on my friends, not on us. And that's a good thing."

Lori drew her knees to her chest and rested her chin on them. "I just want this to be over," she said, tears forming in her eyes. "I want to go home."

"I know," Janet said quietly. "You've held up really well, but don't give up now. Sheriff Reynolds and the others are right outside. They'll figure out how to take Darrin and Bart down."

Lori nodded, then turned her head to rest her cheek on her knees. "I'm glad they're near by, but I don't want anyone else to get hurt because of me."

"Lori, look at me. This isn't your fault. These are bad men who've been causing havoc across three states. I'm sorry you had to be involved, but the sheriff needed to stop them with or without you. When they took you, they made a huge mistake. We weren't about to let them get away with you. Because of you, we knew where they were and were able to track them. Because of you, we're going to put them away for a long time."

A single tear slid down Lori's cheek. "Nothing will ever be the same," she whispered. "They killed Beauty and shot Charlie."

"Charlie will heal," Janet said. "So will your family. It may take a while before you feel safe riding out on your land again, but it will happen." She laid a hand on Lori's arm and met her gaze. "You have to *make* it happen. Otherwise, they win. Don't let them ruin your life, Lori. Don't let them win."

Lori took a deep breath, let it out slowly, and sat up straight, folding her legs tailor fashion. "I won't. I'll raise another horse and I'll ride wherever I damn well please. I won't be haunted by this memory."

"Good for you!"

"Now, what do we need to do to be ready for rescue?"

Janet smiled and nodded. "Let's review our thoughts on using your self-defense techniques offensively. We're going to attack Darrin as soon as we hear my friends make their move."

Lori studied Darrin. "Two to one. We can do this."

"Yes. We can."

34

THE STRIKE

When all three teams were ready, Jason gave the signal to move out. Immediately, Steve began to throw rocks, his excellent pitching arm and dead aim causing the sniper to peek out of his nest. Evan took that opportunity to shoot at the man, who then popped back behind the boulder. Hank piled more rocks beside Steve.

With the sniper engaged, Eli led Eric and Roger away from their protective boulders and across the hillside to try to get a bead on the sniper from the far side. At the same time, Adam, Liam, and Jason stepped quietly from behind their boulders and began their trek uphill to their position above the cave.

Jason marveled at how silently Adam moved. The man made less noise than fallen leaves drifting across a wooded path. Shaking his head at his own attempts, Jason worked to mimic Adam's movements.

His team had just moved into position when Jason's walkie talkie clicked twice. Adam raised an eyebrow at him and Jason nodded. Team 2 was in position as well.

Jason was ready to signal Eli's team to storm the sniper nest when he heard yells and scuffling from inside the cave.

"Janet," he whispered, "what are you doing?"

———

Janet and Lori had watched silently as Bart and Darrin switched places. She cursed silently. She and Lori stood a much better chance of overpowering Darrin than they did with Bart. The man was built like a tank. A big tank.

Before she could rethink their plan, shots rang out and they heard Darrin cursing loudly from outside the cave. Bart knelt by the entrance calling out to his partner for information on what was happening.

Janet moved from sitting cross-legged into a sprinter's crouch. Lori followed suit. Each of them grabbed the rock they'd chosen as a weapon. The women exchanged a steely-eyed glance and Janet nodded.

"We can do this," she said quietly, and the two women raced across the room to tackle Bart.

The man turned just as they reached him, giving Janet a perfect shot at his temple. She pulled her arm back and hit him with the full force of her body behind the blow. The rock connected with his temple and he fell back onto his backside, eyes glazed.

Lori dropped her rock, got behind Bart and locked her right arm around his neck, stabilizing her hold with her left hand and arm. She screamed as he raised his hands and scrabbled at her arm, his nails biting into her flesh.

Janet yelled and pummeled his mid-section, aiming for Bart's liver and solar plexus.

The big man used one hand to try to pry Lori's arm from his neck, while attempting to deflect Janet's punches with the other. Janet could tell he was weakening. Lori might not be completely shutting off his air, but her hold was strong enough to be a problem to him. His face was purpling. Not as fast as

Janet had hoped, but his efforts to throw them off were weakening.

They just had to hold on a little longer. If they could do that, he'd be out cold.

———

Jason grabbed his radio and clicked it three times, the signal for Eli and his team to attack the sniper. He motioned for Adam and Liam to crawl closer.

When all three men were on their bellies above the entrance to the cave, heads close together, he whispered, "Sounds like Janet is staging her own attack. We need to get in there and help her out."

Adam nodded to the sniper, still in full view and lit by the firelight coming from inside the cave. "If we go now, we're going to get shot."

They listened to the yells emanating from the cave below them while keeping an eye on the sniper. He'd obviously heard the scuffle too as he was alternating his focus between the boulders where Jason's first team still sheltered and the entrance to the cave. He wasn't so much as glancing to the far side of his nest, where Eli's team was readying for the fight.

That was good. The sniper wasn't yet aware of his danger from Eli's team.

At least, he hadn't been. There was a lull in the barrage of rocks and bullets from Steve and Evan, giving the sniper a chance to look around. Eli, Roger, and Eric were practically on top of him! The sniper yelled, dropped his rifle, and before Jason or anyone else could even think of shooting him, rolled forward to the cave's entrance and inside.

"All right, men," Jason yelled. "Let's get in there and rescue the women!"

Adam and Liam dropped to the entrance and, following the

sniper's lead, rolled inside. Eli, Eric, and Roger followed right behind. Jason was the last man through the entrance and when he gained his footing and took in the interior of the cave, he froze.

The sniper clutched Janet to his chest, a knife to her throat, while Lori held his partner in a choke hold.

Jason's men ranged in a semi-circle around the perps, not sure what to do.

This was not the sight Jason wanted to see.

35

LAST STAND

Darrin's breath exploded in a curse. He'd nearly been captured by lawmen he hadn't even seen coming. He'd managed to roll to safety, only to discover neither he nor Bart were safe!

Grabbing his knife from its sheath at his belt, he dragged Janet off of Bart, held her firmly against his chest, and set the edge of his knife to her throat.

"Take your hands off of Bart, little girl, or I'll slit her throat."

Lori glared at him, but didn't release her hold on Bart's throat. "You wouldn't dare," she said, "not with the sheriff and the rest of her friends right outside."

Darrin showed his teeth in a feral grin. "You don't have a clue what I'd do." He pressed the knife closer to Janet's skin, nicking her throat and causing a small trickle of blood to run down her neck. "Are you willing to bet her life that I won't do it?"

Lori eased her hold on Bart fractionally, but the big man remained still, his breath rasping.

Before Darrin could push his advantage, men began coming through the low entrance. Darrin dragged Janet back a few paces, turning to face the newcomers.

"Shit," he said under his breath. He now stood even with where Lori sat on the floor with Bart in a headlock, but facing the lawmen so that he could see everyone. He'd rather have had his back to a wall, but at least he knew no one could sneak up on him.

The last man through the entry stood, and immediately froze. His gaze darted from Janet to Lori and back.

"Are you okay, Janet?" he asked.

"So far," she answered.

Darrin's glance flicked to Lori. The dratted girl had tightened her choke hold on Bart again now that she had backup. Darrin needed her to release Bart; he needed Bart to get his breath back and his wits about him. If Bart had Lori at knife point, they might have the leverage they'd need to get out of this alive.

But Bart wasn't going to be any help. He'd have to leave his partner behind. Too bad, they'd made a good team.

Darrin might be facing down six armed lawmen, but he had the advantage, and he knew it. None of them would risk Janet's life to try to take him in. Getting through that low entrance with a hostage would be tricky, but he'd manage it.

They'd have Bart, and they'd've rescued Lori, but Darrin would get away.

And Janet? He hoped he wouldn't have to kill her, but if he did she would've served her purpose. He'd be free to disappear into the wilderness again.

———

Jason studied the man holding a knife to Janet's throat. His hand was steady, but his eyes were wild. He was desperate, and desperate men did stupid things. Like killing a sheriff's deputy right in front of her team. Jason wouldn't allow that to happen. He couldn't. Not only was Janet a valued employee, she was also a friend. One who had stood by him through some rough times.

He glanced at the second man, the one Lori had in a choke hold on the floor of the cave. The man was out of it, and if the purple tinge to his skin was any indication, he didn't have much time left. Jason could deal with that, but he could also use it as a bargaining chip with Janet's assailant.

"I'm leaving now," Janet's assailant said, "and she's coming with me. Nobody move." He dragged Janet forward a step before Jason spoke.

"I think you'd better let Lori move," Jason said. "If she doesn't release your partner, he's going to suffocate."

Lori looked startled, but didn't ease her hold.

"What's your name? It's easier to talk if we know each other. I'm Jason."

"We don't have anything to talk about," the man growled. He glanced at Lori quickly, then focused back on Jason. "Let go of him, girl. Bart's no danger to you now. Not with all these lawmen here."

Lori released Bart, rolled to the side, and jumped to her feet. She raced to Jason's side.

"Eric," Jason said, holding the trembling girl to his side. "Take Lori out of the cave."

Eric scowled, but stepped forward, took Lori's arm gently, and helped her through the low cave entrance. "It's okay," Jason heard him murmur. "You're safe now."

Once Lori was outside, Jason gazed at Janet. She gave him a wry smile before blinking slowly. He wanted to grin, but held it in. Janet had a plan, he just needed to hold Darrin's attention.

He nodded toward Bart. "So, if that's Bart Blakesley, you must be Darrin Haskin."

Darrin grunted. "Not your concern. I told you I'm leaving, and if you want her to live, you'll get out of my way."

The five remaining lawmen held their positions.

"We're not moving," Jason said, "and you're not going anywhere." He smiled. "Except to prison."

Janet moved so quickly even Jason was startled, and he'd expected her to do something.

She grabbed Darrin's knife arm, one of her hands on his hand, the other on his arm, and yanked down. With his forearm and hand locked to her chest, she rotated toward him, dropping and bending until his elbow was jacked up and the knife was pointed at him. She didn't force him to stab himself, though she could have.

Jason jumped forward, forced the knife from the man's hand while Janet released him and stepped back. Roger moved in to support Janet, and Eli helped Jason push Darrin onto the hard stone of the cave floor and cuff him. Adam and Liam rushed to Bart's side, rolled him over, and cuffed him as well.

Once both perps were secure, Jason stepped over to Janet, caught her shoulders in both hands, and studied her, noting the blood on her neck. "Are you hurt?"

Janet touched the bloody spot and smiled grimly. "Not really. It's no worse than what you guys do to yourselves shaving."

Jason nodded. "That was some move. Learn that at the dojo?"

"Nope. That was a self-defense move. I've been teaching it for years at the community center."

"Well, now you have real world experience to tell your students about. Beautifully executed, by the way."

"Thanks. Lori and I had been going over self-defense tactics and how they could be used against these guys." She took a deep breath, let it out slowly, and said, "She did a great job subduing Bart. We'd hoped Darrin would be our target, but it was Bart who was in here when you guys made your move. That meant Bart was the one we had to tackle. She didn't even blink, just moved right in like a trooper."

Jason dropped his hands from her shoulders and motioned her toward the exit. They left the cave, leaving Eli, Liam, Roger, and Adam to get the perps outside.

Eric and Lori joined them, and Lori threw her arms around Janet and sobbed.

"I'm so glad you're safe!" the young woman cried. "I was terrified he'd kill you!"

Janet patted Lori's back. "Well, he didn't. I used the *fingers, shrug, and duck* move to get out of his hold."

Lori's eyes widened. "It worked? Just like you said it would?"

Janet laughed. "It did. I've practiced it enough in classes that I'd've been embarrassed if it hadn't!"

Jason shook his head. "You ladies did a great job on those two. But Lori, be careful. If you're ever in that kind of situation again, don't get cocky. Only use moves you're confident you can handle."

Lori nodded. "Don't worry, Sheriff. I know I couldn't have done what I did in there if I hadn't had Janet to lean on." She met Janet's gaze. "I'll be signing up for every single self-defense class you teach. You'll get sick of seeing me."

Janet put her arm around Lori's shoulders. "Not likely. You'll give the other students confidence. Heck, you'll probably end up teaching some of the classes."

Steve, Hank, and Evan joined them, and Evan said, "Looks like we missed all the fun."

Jason took off his Stetson and wiped his forehead on his shirtsleeve. "I don't know about *fun*, but we definitely saw some action. You guys did your part by helping us get to the cave in the first place."

Janet moved to Hank's side and touched his wounded shoulder briefly. "Glad to see you're up and around, Hank. I was worried Steve wouldn't get to you in time."

"I'm fine," he said quietly, "or at least I will be once we get back to civilization. Are you all right? I've been worried about you."

She touched her neck again. "I'm fine. Lori and I are both fine. Thanks to all of you."

Jason called Eric over. "Find me that sat phone, will you, Eric?"

"Got it right here. Want me to call Clara?"

Jason shook his head. "No. I'll take care of it." He glanced around and caught Eli's eye. "Eli! Do you have a sat phone?"

Eli nodded. "I do."

"Would you call your people and see if you can find us transportation out of here?"

"I can do that."

Jason took the sheriff's department phone from Eric, but before making the call to Clara, he said, "Okay, men. Assignments. Eric, Adam, and Liam, inventory the contents of the cave. Roger and Evan, guard our prisoners. Steve, check out the women and the perps. Make sure there aren't any injuries we're unaware of. Hank, assist Steve." He clapped his hands. "Let's get to work, people."

When everyone settled to their tasks, Jason stepped aside to call Clara. She needed to know what was going on in order to field questions, and he needed to know that things in Garnet Gateway were under control. That his dispatcher wasn't under siege and hadn't needed to call in reinforcements from Sheriff Porter over in Dawes County.

He could hardly wait to get back to his office and business as usual!

36

KRISTI LUNDRIGAN REYNOLDS

Kristi was standing at the cutting table in her quilt shop, *Delectable Mountain Quilting*, measuring fabric for a customer when her cell phone rang. Pulling it from the pocket of her long patchwork skirt, she checked the read-out. Clara, the dispatcher for the sheriff's department was calling.

Glancing at her customer, Kristi said, "Would you excuse me for a moment, Anna? I need to take this call."

"Of course. I'm in no hurry." Anna Marsten was a loyal customer. She'd been especially loyal since Kristi had helped foil a con man's scheme to defraud Anna's mother-in-law out of their ranch. Now the blonde, blue-eyed woman moved back to the shelves to finger more fabric while Kristi focused on what Clara had to say.

"Jason called me at the crack of dawn. He asked me to call you too, but I wanted to wait until business hours," Clara began. "They've captured the kidnappers and Lori and Janet are fine. So is everyone else."

"Oh," Kristi said, breathing a sigh of relief. "Any idea when they'll make it back to town?"

"Jason said the law enforcement rangers were working on transportation, but he didn't have any details yet."

"Will he be heading straight to the detention center?"

Clara was silent for a moment. "He didn't say for sure, but I'd bet someone will bring the bad guys here to the detention center, while the rest head to the hospital. I know he'll want both Lori and Janet to be checked out medically and then there's the one ranger who was shot. He'll need to be looked at as well."

Kristi closed her eyes and nodded though she knew Clara couldn't see her. "Okay, well, please keep me informed."

"You know I will," Clara said. "The minute I have any details, I'll call."

"Thank you, Clara."

When she ended the call, Kristi glanced around to find both her clerks—Ruby and Andrea—as well as Anna staring at her. She smiled.

"Everything's all right," she said. "The bad guys are in custody. Janet and Lori are safe. And no one else has been hurt."

Ruby expelled the breath she'd been holding in a long sigh.

Andrea, looking a bit paler than normal, collapsed into the overstuffed chair they kept near the window for bored husbands.

Anna said, "Oh! Thank heavens. We've been worried about that girl." The Marsten ranch shared a fence line with the Richardsons' Circle R. Ranch families stuck together. "I know Ethan has been beside himself with Lori missing and Charlie shot. He'll be so relieved to have her home safe."

Kristi nodded. "I'm sure he will." Gesturing to Ruby, she asked, "Ruby, will you please help Anna with her purchase. Andrea and I need a minute."

"Of course. Take all the time you need. Anna and I will be fine."

Motioning for Andrea to join her, Kristi led the way to the back of the shop to their kitchen / break room.

"Sit down, Andrea. You look like you might faint." Pulling a glass from the cabinet above the sink, Kristi poured a glass of cold water from the pitcher in the refrigerator and handed it to her clerk. "Drink. It'll help."

Andrea accepted the glass of water and sipped carefully. "I don't know why I'm reacting like this," she said quietly. "It's good news. Lori's safe. Charlie's on the mend. No one else was hurt." She looked at Kristi with wide eyes. "Why do I feel like this?"

Kristi sat across the table from her. "Don't worry about it, Andrea. You've been under a lot of stress and hearing that the ordeal is over has probably released hormones that you've been working to suppress. Just sit still, drink that water, and allow yourself to relax."

"Thanks, Kristi," Andrea said, taking another sip of water. "Do you know when they'll get back?"

Kristi shook her head. "Not yet, but Clara will call when she has details." They sat quietly for a minute before Kristi continued, "I'll be going to meet Jason. Do you want to come with me?"

"Could I?"

"Of course. If Jason is headed for the detention center, I'll wait for him in his office. But I could drop you by the hospital. That's where they'll be taking Lori... and anyone else who needs medical attention."

Andrea nodded. "That would be great. Thank you."

"You sit still until you feel ready to come back to the front," Kristi said, patting Andrea's hand. "I'll just go bring Ruby up to date on our plans."

Kristi walked back to the front of her shop, greatly relieved. Her husband would be home tonight. As would Lori Richardson and Janet Millson.

Somehow, she doubted Janet was going to feel up to hosting a barbecue Saturday night. No matter, the get-together could easily be rescheduled. What mattered was that life would be returning to normal soon.

37

ETHAN RICHARDSON

E than Richardson paced the hallway outside his son's hospital room. Charlie was improving rapidly and the doctor expected he'd be able to go home tomorrow. That was good news, and Ethan was thrilled, but he was even more excited about the news Clara Dahl, the dispatcher for the sheriff's department, had given him.

Lori was safe! The sheriff was bringing her home. And as far as Ethan knew, she hadn't been molested.

He leaned against the wall and breathed a sigh of relief. By this time tomorrow, he might have all three of his children home, safe and sound. Of course, he realized that Lori had been through an ordeal. She would need time to heal from the trauma of being kidnapped and dragged into the wilderness by those horrible men, but she'd be home. She'd be able to heal surrounded by her family… and her community.

He shook his head and continued pacing. Hard to believe that it had all started just a little over twenty-four hours ago. It felt like Lori had been gone for weeks, if not months. Time was a funny thing. When everything was flowing along normally, it felt like time flew. But in a time of crisis, it seemed to slow down and move like a fly caught in honey. Was that supposed to help him see opportunities and make decisions quickly? He didn't think so. No, it seemed more like the slowing only increased his stress. Gave him more time to examine every mistake he'd ever made with one of his children.

A nurse approached with a cart bearing Charlie's lunch. Ethan followed her into his son's room.

"Here you go, Charlie," she said cheerfully. "You're doing well enough that you've graduated to solid food." She placed the food tray on the overbed table and moved it into position for him. "Enjoy!"

As soon as she was gone, Luke reached over a took the lid off Charlie's meal. Grinning at his brother, he said, "Mmm-mmm. Hospital food at its finest!"

Charlie's lunch consisted of what looked like a small hamburger patty, mashed potatoes, a spoonful of mixed vegetables, and for dessert, a vanilla pudding cup.

Examining his meal, Charlie sighed. "Well, at least it's not chicken broth and jello like last night."

"Don't worry, son," Ethan said, "we'll have you home soon and will feed you up good and proper." He turned to Luke, who was still grinning and shaking his head. "Why don't you head on down to the cafeteria, Luke. Grab something to eat. Maybe bring something back for me. I don't want to miss seeing the sheriff."

Luke sobered. "I can't believe they found Lori and are bringing her home." Glancing at his father, he amended his comment. "I mean, of course they're bringing her home! I just thought it would take longer."

"Thank heavens it didn't," Charlie said after swallowing a bite of mashed potatoes.

"About that food, Luke?"

Ethan's eldest backed toward the door. "No problem, Dad. I'll go right now."

"He didn't mean that like it sounded, Dad," Charlie said quietly, not meeting Ethan's eyes.

Ethan sighed. "I know, son. We're all on edge. Nothing is coming out the way we mean it to."

Charlie nodded. "Do... do you think she's all right?"

"We'll find out soon enough." Ethan met Charlie's gaze. "Eat your lunch and try not to worry. I'll be in the hallway if you need me."

"I won't, but don't wear yourself out pacing, Dad."

Ethan gave his son a wry grin and stepped into the hall. So much for keeping his agitation to himself. He'd barely turned to start his pacing when a voice hailed him.

"Ethan! Have you heard anything yet?" Kristi Reynolds and Andrea Jansson hurried down the hall to join him.

"Not yet. Clara said noonish. I'm guessing any time now."

Kristi nodded and held up a bag marked *Roasted Beans'* logo. The Main Street coffee shop was a go-to source of sandwiches and cookies. "Hungry?"

Ethan shook his head. "I just sent Luke down to the cafeteria to find us some food. I'll wait for him." He glanced at Andrea, who also held a *Roasted Beans* bag. The young woman had been a source of strength during Charlie's ordeal. He sincerely hoped his younger son would find the courage to tell her how he felt about her. But that was their problem. Ethan had enough of his own.

"Charlie is eating his lunch," he told Andrea, "if you want to join him. He's got actual food this time."

She smiled at him. "Thanks, Mr. Richardson." And disappeared into Charlie's room.

"I take it Sheriff Reynolds is coming here first?"

"He is," Kristi answered. "Two of his deputies and one of the law enforcement rangers are escorting the criminals to the detention center. They'll have the center's on-call doctor check the men out. Jason didn't want them here with your family and all the other civilians."

She paused, then grinned at Ethan. "You may be surprised to hear that the only injury either of those men sustained was caused by Lori. She evidently had the big man in a choke hold when Jason and his men stormed the cave where they were holed up."

Ethan stumbled back, as though Kristi had shoved him. "Lori? My Lori? She attacked one of those men?"

Kristi nodded. "That's what Clara told me." She turned, stared toward the hospital's entrance, then started walking. "We'll find out soon enough. They're here!"

Jogging a few steps to catch up to Kristi, Ethan soon passed her... and saw his daughter in the midst of a group of armed men and one other woman. All of them looked tired and scruffy, but pleased. Sheriff Reynolds walked between the women looking confident and in charge, despite the dirt on his clothes and the day's growth of beard.

"Here she is, Ethan," Jason said. "She'll need to be checked out..." He stopped mid-sentence as Ethan ignored him and pulled Lori into a bear hug.

"You're back," he said, barely able to choke out the words, tears streaming down his face. "You're safe? They didn't hurt you?"

Lori laughed and cried simultaneously, burrowing into her father's embrace. "I'm fine, Daddy," she said, choking some herself. "I hurt them worse than they hurt me."

Ethan held her at arms' length and studied her face. "Good for you, baby. Good for you!"

"No one's going to take her away from you, Ethan," Jason said, his arm around Kristi, her head resting on his shoulder, "but we need to get her and Janet and Hank signed in so the doctors can take a look at them."

"Of course," Ethan mumbled, keeping an arm around his daughter's waist. "Lead on."

They'd just moved to the registrar's cubicle when Luke came running down the hall. "Lori! You're here! Oh my GOD! Charlie's gonna bust a gut that he can't get out of bed and come hug you!" He pulled his sister away from his Dad and hugged her tightly enough that he lifted her off her feet.

"Easy there, son," Ethan said, adding his arms to make it a group hug. "She'll see Charlie as soon as the doctor looks her over."

Jason smiled at the happy family, kissed Kristi on the cheek, and moved in to the registrar's cubicle to make sure the hospital was aware of their needs and that this was sheriff's department business.

They might be tired, hungry, and dirty, but the lawmen had all done their jobs. Lori Richardson had been found and rescued, and his search party, while a little battered, had come through the experience intact.

This was a good day.

EPILOGUE

K risti carried the large bag into her kitchen and placed it on the counter before leaning down to pet the cats that were alternating between rubbing against her legs and winding around her ankles.

"Not to worry, kitty-kids," she said with a laugh, "I haven't forgotten your dinner." Stepping carefully around Stitches and Between, she opened the cabinet and grabbed a bag of kibble. Pouring it into their dishes, she said, "And since this is a very special day, I'll even let you have a portion of tuna."

Jason came through the back door as she said that and froze. Had he forgotten an occasion? He didn't think so. Frowning, he asked, "What's so special about today?"

She grinned at him as he hung his keys on the peg beside the door. "I'll tell you over dinner. Go get washed up, and get rid of your badge and gun. You're home now."

As he moved across the kitchen, he noticed the bag on the counter. Sniffing the air, he savored the aroma of tomato sauce and perfectly spiced beef. Pausing, he asked, "Rizzoli's? What's the occasion?"

Kristi waved him out of the kitchen. "You'll find out soon enough."

He grumbled, but strode toward the bedroom to do as he'd been asked.

Kristi turned to the cabinet, pulled out dishes and silverware and then unpacked the bag of food. Opening the containers, she slid a generous serving of spaghetti and meatballs onto one plate and lasagna onto the other. By the time Jason returned, she had both meals on the table along with a basket of Rizzoli's fresh-baked focaccia bread and glasses of iced tea.

Quiet reigned as both of them dug into their meals. Spaghetti and meatballs was Jason's favorite Italian dinner, while Kristi loved the perfectly spiced beef, rich tomato sauce, and gooey cheese of Mama Rizzoli's lasagna.

After a few bites, Jason met Kristi's gaze. "Okay, spill. What are we celebrating?"

Kristi fairly beamed. "Andrea had news today," she said, then paused for dramatic effect. "Charlie Richardson asked her to marry him!" Another pause, though this one was very brief. "She said yes, of course."

Jason grinned. "Good for him! And it only took him two months to do what anyone with eyes could see was inevitable back when he was in the hospital."

Kristi swatted his arm, but grinned. "I think they've been in love for years, but it took the ordeal of the kidnapping and shooting to make them realize that life can be terribly unpre-dictable."

Jason cut into a meatball and raised a bite to his lips. Holding it before his lips, he said, "Speaking of that crime, I have news too." He ate the bite of meatball while Kristi waited impatiently.

"And…" she prodded.

"Prosecuting Attorney Nancy Vanderhaven called me today. She met with Haskin and Blakesley and their public defenders and offered them a deal."

"She didn't!" Kristi cried.

Jason nodded. "Don't worry. This turns out well." He grabbed a piece of focaccia bread, dragged it through some excess spaghetti sauce, and popped it in his mouth. After swallowing, he picked up his glass of tea and took a healthy swig.

Kristi was ready to strangle him before he finally spoke again.

"She pointed out the preponderance of evidence her office had accumulated, the numerous charges both men were facing, and offered to not seek the death penalty, but instead ask the judge to be lenient so that they could seek parole after twenty years or so."

"Okay, they'll be locked up for at least twenty years. That's not as bad as I was imagining. What do they have to do?"

"Plead guilty to all charges." He took another bite. "Her deal saves the taxpayers the cost of a jury trial. Which, as she pointed out to them, they were unlikely to win. In a ranching community like Garnet County, the fact that they shot Lori's mare, a horse she'd hand-raised from a foal, would likely ensure their conviction."

Kristi nodded. "When will you find out their decision?"

"That's just it. That's the reason Vanderhaven called. It's all done. Fait accompli. They pled guilty to Judge Evers, and…." Now it was Jason's turn to employ a dramatic pause. "He rejected PA Vanderhaven's deal."

Kristi sucked in a breath, then exhaled explosively. "He could do that?"

"Yep. Totally within the judge's authority. He not only rejected the plea deal, he found them guilty on all counts and remanded them to the custody of the Montana State Prison in Deer Lodge to live out their sentences. Consecutive sentences, not concurrent. And we're talking life sentences here." He took another drink of tea. "They'll never come up for parole. Not the way Judge Evers set them up."

"Oh, wow," Kristi said with a shake of her head. "I didn't see that coming."

Jason nodded. "No one did. PA Vanderhaven was shocked."

They cleared the table after dinner, cleaned up the kitchen, and were headed toward the living room to watch a little television when Jason's cell phone rang.

He glanced at the display and shrugged. "It's Anita. I have to answer it."

Kristi nodded with good grace.

"Sheriff Reynolds." He listened for a few moments, then said, "Tell Carl I'll be there as quickly as I can. Call Evan and Roger and have them meet me at the Marsten ranch."

After he ended the call, he pulled Kristi into his arms and kissed her thoroughly. "Sorry, honey, but I have to go."

"Of course you do. Is everyone all right at the Broken M," she asked.

Jason strode into the bedroom to buckle on his gun belt and replace his badge. "As far as I know," he answered when Kristi followed him. "A riderless horse wandered into their paddock. When they checked the animal out, they found blood on the saddle." He glanced at her again. "They need me to determine whether or not it looks like a crime has been committed."

Kristi sighed. "I'd been enjoying the break in dangerous events."

He smiled grimly. "Me too, but we don't know what this is yet."

"Just promise me you'll be careful, and that you'll come home soon."

"I always do," he said and kissed her cheek as he moved past. "And I always will."

Kristi nodded and gave him a smile. What else could she do? She was the sheriff's wife. But as he walked away from her, she whispered, "Be safe."

Jason strode to the back door, grabbed his keys from their peg, and left his home behind. Off to serve and protect his friends and constituents: the good people of Garnet County, Montana.

ALSO BY DEBBIE MUMFORD

Kristi Lundrigan Mysteries:

- DELECTABLE MOUNTAIN QUILTING (NOVEL)
- IN A PICKLE (NOVEL)
- DOUBLE WEDDING RING (NOVEL)
- FOOL'S PUZZLE (SHORT STORY)
- WILDFIRE! (SHORT STORY)
- CHRISTMAS STAR (SHORT STORY)
- KRISTI LUNDRIGAN MYSTERIES BUNDLE

Sheriff Reynolds Mysteries:

- ABDUCTED! (NOVEL)
- WISH FULFILLMENT (SHORT STORY)

Gus and Ghost Short Story Series:

- SEVENTH
- SEVENTH: FIRST FRUITS
- DEATH OF AN ALCHEMIST (UNCOLLECTED ANTHOLOGY)
- SEVENTH: THE SAMHAIN DILEMMA
- DARK OF THE MOON (UNCOLLECTED ANTHOLOGY)
- FLIGHT PLAN (UNCOLLECTED ANTHOLOGY)
- MIDSUMMER NIGHT (UNCOLLECTED ANTHOLOGY)

Logans of Lastalrig Series:

- HER HIGHLAND LAIRD (NOVELLA)
- HER HIGHLAND YULE (SHORT STORY)
- WISE WOMAN (SHORT STORY)
- CHOCOLATE COMFORT (A VERY SHORT PREQUEL)

Red's Series:

- RED'S MAGICK (SHORT STORY COLLECTION)
- THE GHOST IN THE GLASS (SHORT STORY)
- SEEING RED (SHORT STORY)

Signs of the Prophecy Novels:

- YOUNGEST
- SEEKER
- CHOSEN (COMING SOON!)

Sorcha's Children Series:

- SORCHA'S HEART (NOVELLA)
- DRAGONS' CHOICE (NOVEL)
- DRAGONS' FLIGHT (NOVEL)
- DRAGONS' DESIRE (NOVEL)
- DRAGONS' DESTINY (NOVEL)
- SORCHA'S CHILDREN (AN EPIC FANTASY SERIES BUNDLE)

Supernatural Yellowstone Short Story Series:

- REALITY BITES
- THE CAT LADY OF YELLOWSTONE

Uncollected Anthology Short Stories:

- DEATH OF AN ALCHEMIST (UA ALCHEMY)
- THE WEDDING CAKE (UA MAGICAL ARTS)
- DARK OF THE MOON (UA PARANORMAL PIRATES)
- IN THE BANYAN COPSE (UA UNEXPECTED HISTORIES)
- OLD ONE (UA MAGICAL QUESTS)
- HAVE HOARD, WILL SEEK (UA A DIVERSITY OF DRAGONS)
- FLIGHT PLAN (UA MYSTICAL MAPS)
- DISAPPEARED! (UA WERE-CREATURES & CONUNDRUMS)
- MIDSUMMER NIGHT (UA SUMMER SOLSTICE)

- WARDEN AND HUNTER (UA MAGICAL LAW)

Universal Star League Short Story Series:

- VOYAGES INTO THE BLACK (COLLECTION)
- THE WARBIRDS OF ABSAROKA
- AWAKENING THE WARRIOR
- INCIDENT ON THE ODYSSEY
- THE QUEEN'S CAPTIVE
- THE LOST COLONY
- FREIGHTER FAMILIES IN SPACE

Witchling Short Story Series:

- WITCHLING
- THE SOLITARY SORCERESS
- TO PROTECT A PRINCESS

Stand Alone Novels:

- SECOND SIGHT

Historical Fiction:

- HER HIGHLAND LAIRD (NOVELLA)
- HER HIGHLAND YULE
- INCIDENT ON THE HIGH LINE
- MISS BAINBRIDGE'S SUMMER ADVENTURE
- MISS BAINBRIDGE'S CHRISTMAS PARTY
- SISTERS IN SUFFRAGE
- THE TRAIL WHERE WE CRIED
- THE WHITE DRAGON AND THE RED

Short Story Collections:

- A FLIGHT OF DRAGONS
- A LOVELY LITTLE CHRISTMAS

- LOVE IN A FLASH
- TALES OF BYGONE DAYS
- TALES OF LOVE & MAGICK
- TALES OF THE UNEXPECTED
- TALES OF TOMORROW
- TALES OF DISASTROUS DEEDS

Short Fiction:

- A GROVE OF MOUNTAIN ASH
- A WALK WITH GEORGIA
- AN ALIEN ADVENTURE
- ASTROMANCER
- BECAUSE OF THE CHRISTMAS STROLL
- BENEATH AND BEYOND
- DEEP DREAMING
- DELIA'S DECISION
- EGG THIEF
- ENCHANTMENT, INC.
- GOD-TOUCHED
- ICE
- ICE STORM
- INCIDENT ON THE HIGH LINE
- IN SEARCH OF A VALENTINIAN
- IZZIE
- JOLLY WELL DONE
- KEYSTROKES & INTUITION
- MISS BAINBRIDGE'S CHRISTMAS PARTY
- MISS BAINBRIDGE'S SUMMER ADVENTURE
- NEEDLE-GREEN
- NEW YEAR
- OPENING HER EYES
- REMEMBRANCE
- SILVER-TIPPED DEATH
- SIMON SAYS
- SISTERS IN SUFFRAGE
- SKYE DREAMS

- SMOKEJUMPER
- SPINNING
- THE FAMILIAR
- THE TIE THAT BINDS
- THE TRAIL WHERE WE CRIED
- THE WHITE DRAGON AND THE RED
- TO DREAM OF FLYING
- TREASURES
- TRIAL ON THE TRAIL
- WAKINYAN'S VALLEY

"WDM Presents" Anthologies:

- SPUN YARNS UNWOUND, VOL. 1
- SPUN YARNS UNWOUND: VOL. 2
- SPUN YARNS UNWOUND: VOL. 3
- SPUN YARNS UNWOUND: VOL. 4
- SPUN YARNS UNWOUND: VOL. 5
- TALES OF MYSTERY & MAYHEM
- 2016: A YEAR OF SHORT FICTION
- 2017: A YEAR OF SHORT FICTION
- WDM PRESENTS: SHORT FICTION FROM 2018
- WDM PRESENTS: SHORT FICTION FROM 2019
- WDM PRESENTS: SHORT FICTION FROM 2020
- WDM PRESENTS: SHORT FICTION FROM 2021

PREVIEW: DELECTABLE MOUNTAIN QUILTING

If you enjoyed *Abducted!*, you may want to read *Delectable Mountain Quilting*, a quilt themed cozy mystery set in Garnet Gateway, Montana. Here's a sample chapter.

———

Kristiana Lundrigan, Kristi to her friends and family, stared out the picture window beside her breakfast table. She adored the view, showing as it did the majestic Absaroka Range, including Mount Cowen, the highest peak visible from her Paradise Valley home. Scooping the last bite of scrambled eggs onto her fork, she concentrated on allowing the peace of the mountain scenery to soothe her soul. Today would be exciting, perhaps even nerve-wracking. She wanted to start it as calmly as possible.

Her small house sat on the eastern edge of Garnet Gateway, Montana, giving her an unimpeded view of the open valley as it approached the foothills of the 'Sorkees. Kristi had known it was the home she'd been searching for the moment she saw it. Single story, three bedrooms, and a nicely updated bathroom with an old fashioned claw footed tub. The view from the breakfast nook had been the cherry on top as far as Kristi was concerned.

She'd converted the east facing bedroom into a quilting studio, leaving the other two for a guest bedroom and her own use.

Designing her studio had been a delight. She'd finally had the space to create a floor-to-ceiling design wall by installing sheets of flannel-covered Homasote board on the largest unbroken wall. The flannel was the perfect touch. No need to pin her blocks to the wall (though the Homasote board was porous enough to allow for that if needed), they adhered to the flannel effortlessly.

Her sewing table, with its state-of-the-art Viking machine, sat in front of the room's only window, with the large cutting table on her left and the design wall to her right. Her ironing station stood behind her, near the closet, which had had its sliding doors removed and shelves built in to hold Kristi's fabric stash, stored quilts, and as-yet-unfinished projects. The final touch had been turning one of her early quilts into a Roman shade and hanging it over the entrance to the closet, protecting her stash of brightly colored fabric from too much light.

Kristi picked up her mug of mint tea from the scrubbed oak breakfast table and sipped the fragrant brew.

The divorce had been a painful blow, but it was in her past now. She was her own woman at last, with a home that suited her, and— in less than a week!— a business of her own. She was no longer Jason's wife, nor was she her father's little girl. She was

Kristiana Lundrigan, quilter, teacher, and soon-to-be business woman. An upstanding member of the Garnet Gateway community.

Garnet Gateway. She loved this small Montana town, nestled serenely in the Paradise Valley and guarded by the imposing Absaroka Mountains. She wasn't a native, hadn't been born in the town or even on one of the surrounding ranches, but Garnet Gateway was her home. Had been since she followed Jason here after her graduation from Montana State University in Bozeman. She'd been ready to follow him to Denver, where he'd worked his way up from patrol officer to homicide detective, but Jason had chosen to return home to Montana, to Garnet Gateway.

She'd married in Garnet Gateway. Established her first real home here, and had planned to grow old and die here. Still did, as a matter of fact. Only now she was alone.

Well, maybe not *exactly* alone.

As if summoned by her thought, Stitches and Between, her moggy cats, strolled into the kitchen and hopped lightly onto the window seat beside the table to join her. Stitches, the older of the pair, was a gray tabby female with four white paws. Between, named for the tiny, sharp needles used in hand quilting, was a little tuxedo male with the personality of a perennial kitten. Though Stitches was hardly a big cat, she outweighed Between by a good two pounds. The pair were best friends and excellent companions for Kristi.

"Well, good morning, you two," Kristi said, taking a moment to scratch behind first Stitches' ears and then Between's. "What have you been up to while I was eating?"

Stitches settled onto the cushioned window seat, front paws folded beneath her chest, purring contentedly, while Between nipped Kristi's finger gently… always ready to remind her that she was *his* human. He was happy to share her affection with Stitches, of course, but Between was a possessive little fellow.

Kristi nodded. "I love you too, Between." She understood possessive. And loyalty. And trust.

Jason, her ex-husband, had failed in all three areas. He'd had a brief affair during an out of town convention, and while he'd been honest enough to confess (when she confronted him with clear evidence), he'd failed to understand her possessiveness, or her expectation of loyalty, or that he'd forfeited her trust. He'd expected her to forgive and forget and for their lives to continue as if his indiscretion had never happened.

Unfortunately for him, Kristi wasn't built that way. She was too aware of her own worth to allow herself to be treated with such casual disrespect.

None of that changed the fact that she loved him.

Always had.

Always would.

But she'd divorced him anyway.

She refused to live with a man she couldn't trust, so despite a broken heart, she did what needed to be done and moved forward into a new, solitary life.

But when she closed her eyes...

...it was Jason's face that floated to the top of her consciousness.

He might not fit every woman's definition of handsome, but he had always been her gold standard. High forehead, strong jaw, steely gray eyes that could go all soft and almost blue when his emotions were high.

She tried to keep him out of her thoughts, and was mostly successful during the day... but nights were a different matter.

When she climbed into bed each night, usually with a cat curled on either side, she'd dream of Jason. Of running her fingers through his wavy chestnut hair, the thick mass of it like silk between her fingers. Or she'd giggle again as his unshaven chin scratched her cheek after a sensuous night of intimate pleasure.

And... Oh!... did she dream of the pleasures of making love to him!

Only to wake at dawn mourning the loss of the life they'd built together. The life she'd expected to continue until death parted them.

Busyness kept her going. She exorcised Jason from her days by constant activity. Meetings with the divorce attorney. Moving from the home they had shared into an apartment until their affairs (what an appropriate word!) were settled. Designing quilt patterns and then choosing fabrics and making sample blocks. Anything to keep herself from remembering that he had betrayed her. That he didn't love her... or at least didn't love her enough.

When the dust settled and the divorce was final, Kristi found that she had sufficient funds to buy a house in Garnet Gateway. She launched herself into the real estate market, determined to find the perfect home. She knew exactly what she wanted: a small house with enough space for a dedicated quilting studio; and when she found it, she didn't hesitate.

Not quite a year as a single woman and Kristi had taken back her maiden name, bought a home, and adopted Stitches and Between. She'd just begun to think about quitting her part-time secretarial job and establishing a career as a quilt artist when she'd learned that the local quilt shop was for sale.

Talk about perfect timing!

She'd made an appointment with her accountant, crunched some pretty amazing numbers, and determined that the inheritance her maternal grandmother had left her would be enough to not only make the down payment, but would allow for some remodeling if she planned carefully.

Nanna Van Oss would be pleased and proud to know she'd helped Kristi realize her dream of owning her own business, and a quilt shop was an apt use for the money. After all, Nanna was the one who'd taught Kristi to quilt.

Kristi had toured the quilt shop that very day, jotting down ideas for how she would use the space, as well as noting renovations that she'd want to see made. She'd made an offer that same afternoon, and then, praying for a quick acceptance, had begun to load her stitches, nice and even, so that when she pulled the needle through she wouldn't have to stop and pick any of them out.

She'd filled out the application for a small business loan, set up telephone interviews with several contractors, and used her notes to draw up plans for the renovations she hoped to make. With her plans in place, she'd settled back to wait for the current owner's response.

Mattie Stebbings, while not exactly a friend, was someone she knew on sight. Kristi often bought her quilting cottons from Mattie's shop and the women were both members of the statewide quilt guild. Kristi had hoped that Mattie would find her an acceptable beneficiary for the shop.

The wait hadn't been long. Less than twenty-four hours after the offer was made, Mattie accepted. Kristi's small business loan was also approved in short order, and the closing for the quilt shop was fast-tracked. In a mere thirty days, Kristi would own *Delectable Mountain Quilting*!

That was twenty-five days ago. Closing was now only five days away. Come Monday, the shop would be hers.

Time to meet with her chosen contractor and set the wheels in motion.

That was her agenda for today.

She'd arranged to meet Mark Robards, her contractor, at the shop this morning. Mattie, who seemed unusually anxious to consummate the sale, had closed the store as soon as she'd accepted Kristi's offer for the business, which included the building, land, and inventory, so the realtor, Stacy Akins, would also be present. Kristi intended to outline her desired changes and expected Mark to provide a detailed estimate of the cost.

Turning her gaze to the mountains once more, Kristi took a

deep breath, held it for a moment, then released it slowly. Everything was going to work out. She just knew it. Mark would give her a reasonable bid; the remainder of Nanna Van Oss's gift would more than cover the work; and the closing papers would be signed on Monday.

Each stitch in the last twenty-five days had followed the last, neat as a pin. These final steps would as well.

Glancing at the cats, she grinned. "It's going to be an exciting day, kids. You two will soon be quilt store cats!"

————

Look for *Delectable Mountain Quilting* at your favorite online retailer.

ABOUT DEBBIE MUMFORD

Debbie Mumford specializes in speculative fiction (fantasy, paranormal romance, and science fiction) as well as mystery and historical fiction. Author of the popular *Sorcha's Children* series, Debbie loves the unknown, whether it's the lure of space or earthbound mythology. Her work has been published in multiple volumes of *Fiction River*, as well as in *Heart's Kiss Magazine*, *Amazing Monster Tales*, and many other popular anthologies. She writes about dragon-shifters, time-traveling lovers, and detectives—whether amateur or professional—for adults as Debbie Mumford, and science fiction and fantasy for tweens and young adults as Deb Logan.

Join Debbie's special announcement newsletter list and receive a FREE story!

To learn more, visit Debbie at:
debbiemumford.com/

f facebook.com/DebbieMumfordWrites
a amazon.com/author/debbiemumford
BB bookbub.com/authors/debbie-mumford

www.ingramcontent.com/pod-product-compliance
Lightning Source LLC
Chambersburg PA
CBHW022156240626
47153CB00007B/2693